A WESTERN NOVEL

I0626257

The
BIG CORRAL

AL CODY

WILDSIDE PRESS

Copyright, 1948, 1949, by Dou   Mead & Company, Inc.

THE GIRL in pink tights, whose hair was like smoke-filled flame, peeped through a slit in the folds of the curtain, and her voice turned falsetto with excitement.

"He's out there, Marian—the big one who looks like a bear. He's staring all around the room in that way he has—as though the people were the ground he walks on. But it's you he's looking for, of course!"

Marian Breen shrugged one shoulder disdainfully. It was a slender shoulder, the gleam of it rippling like ivory above the deep turkey-red of her dress. She frowned at herself in the mirror, giving an impatient touch to lips already vivid, dark stormy eyes rebellious under hair deep and rich as a miser's gold.

"What did you say his name was, Marian?" the girl in tights persisted. "And where's he from?"

"I didn't say, but he says it's Rawe North, and claims to be from beyond that new cow town of Wichita," Marian answered indifferently. "To hear him tell it, he owns all outdoors—or intends to."

"And he's crazy about you—as who wouldn't be? I'll bet he asks you to marry him tonight! He's got that look on his face!"

"You're too romantic, Altie. That's a look of conquest, not love. What he wants is one big corral with everything he can think of in it—including a woman, if he thinks she'll add anything to his prestige or the value of his ranch. All that he's really interested in is that it shall be *his* corral, the biggest in the country, with the best of everything in it—cows, cayuses, even a woman, All *his!*"

"Maybe," Altie agreed doubtfully. "But what's so bad about that, if you're the woman? If he asks you, you'll say yes, won't you?"

"Will I?" Marian eyed her reflection with a gleam of contempt. "It might depend on how much of it is talk and how much is on the hoof, with his brand on its hide! Such charms as I'm possessed of, which appeal to men, I don't intend to sell cheaply!"

Altie sighed.

"I sure don't blame you, Marian," she agreed. "If I had a face and figure like you've got—and that devil-take-all air to go with it—I'd play hard to get, too. All I've got is a pair of legs and this hair and a line, and the big ones don't go for that. I—oh, there's the other one, Marian! The man who was here months ago. The one who looks like the world was his oyster, and he'd just swallowed it! Now there'll be something doing!"

"What do you mean?" Marian's tone sharpened for just an instant as she swung about. Then she had control of herself again; her voice was without a shading of emotion. "Your descriptions, Altie, are colorful, but the way you do run on—"

"You know who I mean, well enough," Altie said imperturbably. "Who else could almost lift you out of your chair to take a look, like us ordinary females? I mean the one who's always smiling and cool, instead of arrogant and cold. The little one—though he's big enough, for he must be close to six feet, even if your Big Corral does top him by three inches. He's got red hair like mine, only more carroty, and he has a smile for every woman—but something extra in it when he looks at you, like you were the pearl in his oyster."

"It sounds as though it might be Tripp Devero," Marian returned. "He's from that same Kansas country. And the first time he ever met me, he told me he was going to marry me—when he got around to it!"

Altie squealed.

"And you talk about men like that as though they came in bunches, like wild cherries!" she protested. "But he looks dangerous, somehow!"

"They're both dangerous," Marian shrugged. "One's from Texas, the other from Tennessee. If they want to kill each other off, that will solve one problem!"

Altie eyed her reproachfully.

"You sound as if you didn't have a heart at all, Marian," she sighed. "And I suppose, if they fought and only one came out alive, you'd take the winner!"

4

"I might," Marian agreed. "Or I might not. If he was big enough to take over his rival's corral with what's in it—maybe!"

Out in front, Rawe North crowded his long legs under an inadequate table and glanced around impatiently. It was soon time for the Golden-Throated Thrush to make her appearance and sing, and the big saloon was filling to capacity, as always, for her act. The Paddle Wheel was the biggest, gaudiest saloon in St. Louis, and in these days the most prosperous, due to its main attraction. A fact of which Pete Hartse, the bull-necked proprietor, was jealously aware.

North could see him now, hovering in the background, keeping a watchful eye on the business. Hartse wore a starched white shirt, smudged and gaping at the neck, and his huge bulk was as incongruous in it as a draft horse would have been seeking to prance and cavort in a ring with Shetland ponies. A four-carat diamond blazed from the middle of the shirt front, another of equal size was on one sausage-like finger.

Hartse looked quickly away as North's eyes ranged to him, and the cattleman smiled grimly. Hartse hated him—they had clashed more than once—and feared him too, of course. Hated and feared him because he was here to take the Thrush away, and Marian Breen was a gold mine. Also, as North suspected, the thick lipped Hartse wanted her for himself. Few women had ever resisted him long. Strange as it seemed, he was counted as a ladies' man, and North had it reliably that the saloon keeper had gone so far as to offer to marry her. To be turned down then, with his wealth, had infuriated him. Though it had not affected his business sense.

Now, of course, he was doubly jealous. North shrugged. Let him start trouble, if he felt that way! He'd killed such men before.

A newcomer was standing near the doorway, looking over the saloon with a quick, bright glance in which amusement seemed to ripple like the sheen of sunshine on the dust haze inside a room. He had spoken no word, made no gesture, but there was a momentary hush as men—and the women of the place no less—turned to look at him. North felt a red flush creeping into his own face. It was always that way when

Tripp Devero entered a room, or any gathering. There was a magnetism about the man of which North was grudgingly jealous.

He studied Devero for a moment, unobserved. Noting the slender gracefulness of him, so that he seemed slighter than he actually was. The reddish hair which added only a touch of clowning to the bitter-bright mockery which seemed always to dwell in his face. Eyes that surveyed the world with that same mirthless humor, quick and sure, like the gun at his hip. If there was a more dangerous man in this room than himself, North knew that it would be Tripp Devero. And the room might be broadened to include the wild turbulence of St. Louis, the sweep of prairieland from Kansas to Texas, and still the same would apply.

There was no doubt in North's mind as to what Devero was here for, so far from their ranches on that branch of the Arkansas where it ran still as a young stream. Both were big men, there in that raw land of west Kansas, and neighbors. Neighbors, in that only land—a hundred miles or so of it— lay between them. Neighbors, but scarcely friends. Only so impelling a reason as Marian Breen could draw Tripp Devero so far from home, as it had done with North himself.

No, they were not friends, nor ever could be. He hated Devero triply—first for encroaching on land which might otherwise have been his for the taking. Second because Devero was here for the same reason as himself, and always because Devero was what he would never be—slender, graceful, assured, always at ease wherever he went. Rawe North was like his name. Big, blunt, rough-edged. He had always been that way and always would be, and he took a fierce pride in being as he was. But deep down the jealousy rankled.

Devero had seen him now. He stared for a moment, faint surprise showing on his face, and then he came across the room, picking his way like a cat among a disorderly rubble. A drunken man clutched at his shoulder, but Devero slid out from under it with smooth assurance. A girl smiled open invitation at him, and he returned the smile with easy good nature and without a pause. Then he stood, looking down at North.

"You're too big a man for these tables, Rawe," he grinned.

6

"And, as usual, I find you underfoot. Though I should have known that you'd be here."

"I've been here a week," North said shortly. "But I'm leaving tomorrow."

"Then we should have a neighborly drink before you go," Devero suggested, and motioned to a bartender. "I'm surprised you've been so long, Rawe."

"I had business," North shrugged. "As for what you've come for—you're too late."

"Maybe." Devero seemed unperturbed. "Time is a funny thing. Like a river. It keeps flowing along, no matter what you do. Sometimes you think you've got it dammed up, but it overflows and goes on. Or you dig a new channel. But pretty soon it cuts its way back. You can fool with it, but you can't stop it."

"But you can't fool with me!" North warned. Such talk bothered him, for he could never quite understand it, but he sensed the meaning and resented it. "I tell you you're too late. I'm going home tomorrow, and I'm taking her with me!"

"Does she know it yet?" There was faint skepticism in Devero's query. North tossed off his drink.

"She'll find it out," he said.

"Just like that, eh? Well, I'll dance at your wedding, Rawe —maybe."

The retort on North's lips was cut off as the curtains parted on the stage. The boisterous room grew suddenly silent, a greater tribute than applause would have been. Altie was there, along with half a dozen girls similarly clad, and they performed a dance which was watched with tolerance as the curtain-raiser. Then, as they trooped off, the Golden-Throated Thrush floated onto the stage.

Float was an apt word. Her dress swept the floor, so that only a toe twinkled briefly beneath it, as the flash of ivory showed at her shoulders. She moved effortlessly, like a leaf in the wind. The deep, tarnished gold of her hair caught and reflected back the lamplight, and she was at once vividly alive, yet as coldly aloof as a sword. It was that sureness in her which most attracted Rawe North. Like himself, she knew what she wanted, and nothing would turn her aside from her purpose.

For a moment she looked out at the rough, now silent

7

crowd, then began to sing. Easy then to tell why she was known the length of the two rivers as the Golden-Throated Thrush, why Hartse had the best business of any saloon in St. Louis.

She sang none of the popular songs which rawed a man's throat like new whiskey, or set his blood aflame in similar fashion. Everyone knew that the Thrush sang only the old songs, those which whispered of home, of half forgotten dreams. Songs that stirred memories which might be painful. Music to tauten the face of a man, to twist his heart. Had any other woman sung them to such a crowd, there would have been harsh and angry protest. But with the Thrush, men paid good gold to listen.

She sang six songs, steeped in the fragrance of memories. Only when she had finished was there a storm of applause. Everyone knew that six was her limit, that there would be no encores, no dances, no drinks with the customers. She was Marian Breen, the Thrush, and men took no liberties with her. But Altie and those who had danced were down on the floor now, to dance or to drink with any who might ask.

Tonight, however, instead of retiring directly behind the curtain, Marian startled her audience by stepping down from the stage, walking directly to the table where two outlanders sat. Here in St. Louis they were outlanders, men from the frontier which was constantly being crowded back, which had lapped like the river at St. Louis not long before, but in a night had been so far removed that those who now habited the town could be recognized as a breed apart. Men stared in surprise, and Hartse scowled and cursed under his breath.

Both men sprang to their feet as she approached and North flicked his newly lit cigar toward a cuspidor. She was smiling at both of them, holding out a hand to each.

"How are you, Rawe?" she said. "And you, Tripp? This is nice, to see you again!"

"That goes double," Devero grinned. "I rode all the way from west Kansas, Marian, to hear you sing again—and to see if you were ready to marry me yet."

"You haven't changed much, have you?" she asked, sinking into a chair while they resumed their own. "The first time you ever saw me, you told me you were going to marry me some day."

8

"I haven't changed my mind about that." Devero retorted. "Your time's my time, but the sooner the better."

"As I've told you, Tripp, you're too late," North reminded him. "I'm startin' back for Kansas tomorrow, and the Rail Road Track. And she's going with me!"

"Am I?" Marian surveyed him with a detached interest. "Why didn't you tell me before?"

"I thought you understood that I intended to marry you," North said impatiently. "And I've been pretty busy with other things."

"We cattlemen have a lot to tend to, Marian," Devero explained with a grin. "Special man like Rawe. He's working to corral himself the biggest ranch in Kansas."

"That's right," North agreed. "I'm going to have the biggest ranch in Kansas—the biggest herds of cattle, the biggest house, the—"

"The biggest wife?" she suggested demurely. "I'm afraid you'd have to feed me a lot of beef steaks to make me that, Rawe."

North colored, uncomfortably suspicious that these two were making sly fun of him.

"Not the biggest wife," he corrected. "The most beautiful—"

He was about to say more, but Hartse was approaching the table, his heavy face black with anger. He gestured with a big thumb toward the dressing rooms.

"Ain't you forgettin' your own rule, Marian?" he demanded. "Not to talk with none of the customers, here on the floor? Get on back!"

"I'm breaking the rule," Marian said coolly, "since this is my last night on your floor, Pete Hartse. I'm through with working for you."

- 2 -

HARTSE STARED, little eyes seeming to recede further into the encompassing folds of flesh. His tone took on an angry rumble.

"Through?" he echoed. "You ain't no such thing through.

You can't quit that way. Now get back to your room, and be quick about it—"

He was reaching pudgy fingers for her white shoulder when North hit him. He came out of his chair like a grizzly charging from its den, and the simile was good even to the way he struck. It was a full-fisted swing with all his pent-up rage behind it, and it smashed Pete Hartse full in the face—flattening his great nose in a red smear, driving him back for half a dozen steps before he could stop.

But it bespoke the caliber of the man to check then as he did, rocking on the balls of his feet. Other men had been hit by Rawe North, but never had he hit a man as he hit Hartse then. But no other man had ever stood up to such a blow.

For a moment Hartse stood, the gore smearing across his face, starting to spatter down onto the soiled white shirt. Then he started forward, and for all the uncouth bulk of him, he moved with the darting quickness of that shaggy beast of the wilderness which he so much resembled, the wolverine. A bellow emitted from his lips, partly of rage and pain, but partly in signal to his own roustabouts—the crew he kept to back his sway here at the Paddle Wheel, to see that no man disputed him and lived.

Alertly Tripp Devero was on his feet, drawing Marian back with him, as the crowd quickly formed a ring around the contestants. Devero's voice was cool, even amused, but it carried with a clear distinctness in the moment of hush following Hartse's roar.

"We'll keep it fair," he warned. "Anybody who interferes I'll kill."

Marian Breen, knowing who the crew were, was quick to observe how swiftly that brought them to a stand. Already they had been starting to crowd forward, to come to the aid of their employer. But it was evident that the reputation of Tripp Devero with a gun was known here as it was from the Rio Grande to the sluggish-flowing Platte. They checked, and Hartse mouthed a contemptuous defiance.

"Sure," he snarled. "I can handle any man that interferes in my business, alone!"

He was reaching with big paws, fingers working hungrily. No man had ever come within the clutch of those fingers and long continued to fight. But Rawe North was not afraid of

10

him. His own blood was at a savage pitch, and here was a chance to show this woman and all others who might be interested, including Tripp Devero, that no man could stand in the way of Rawe North.

North planted himself, one hand against a table. Steadied so, he lifted his foot and kicked. But swift and treacherous as that move was, he had underestimated the speed of his clumsy-looking antagonist. Hartse seemed to pull his protuberant front back, and his hands darted and closed on North's foot. Then he did an incredible thing. He grunted, face purpling with the effort, but he was turning around, lifting North off his other foot and straightening him with the swing. Only when he had made a complete turn, the tempo quickening, North like the outjutting spoke of a wheel, well up off the floor, did he suddenly release his hold.

It was enough. Rawe North sailed through the air for a dozen feet, to crash against a table and overturn it in a smashed welter of bottles and glasses. He hit the floor with a crash which jarred the building, and even as he sprawled there, Hartse was upon him, leaping into the air, both big feet bunched to come down on the sprawled figure beneath.

A gasp went up, for it looked as though nothing could save North. Such a fall would have finished most men. But Rawe North, shaken and badly surprised as he was, was no ordinary man. He managed to roll enough to miss that vicious onslaught, and as he raised up, he was gripping a leg of the smashed table in one hand.

Still lying half sprawled, he smashed out with the clubbed leg, and the snap of it as it broke off short across Hartse's ankle sounded like the pop of a gun. Hartse howled, a stentorian roar to dwarf his earlier yell, and then he lost his footing and sprawled on the floor. Rawe North rolled and was on top of him, slugging at the gory face beneath.

The saloon keeper reached up and got a handful of hair. and his teeth clicked viciously as he dragged North's head down and tried to bite his nose. A heave rolled North off him. and then they came to their feet again and circled warily. each mutually respectful of the other.

Tripp Devero was watching with that amused glint still in his eyes, but his face was watchful as he kept his gaze on the roustabouts. Marian's face showed no more emotion than did his own. Far less than that of the crowd.

They looked to be evenly matched, and it was in Devero's mind that this would be brutal and bloody before it reached its end. North now was taking the offensive. He rushed and swung, and one fist rocked the saloon keeper, landing where his nose was already a bloody smear. But the second blow missed, and Hartse landed in turn, a fair smash to the jaw which staggered North, rocking his head back. Another to the midriff doubled him up, followed by a punch which had him rocking in agony. In that moment victory was with the keeper of the Wheel.

No sympathy showed on the face of Tripp Devero. Rawe North was his rival, and more than that. If Hartse finished him, in a fair fight he had no complaint. A fair fight in this town included few rules. But Hartse was going berserk as he tasted triumph. He had been raised along the waterfront of sundry wharves from New Orleans to Independence, and he knew one sure way to end all quarrels. With his opponent twisted in torment, blinded and helpless for the moment, he prepared to end it in merciless style.

Another gasp went up from the onlookers as they saw the flash of the knife in Hartse's huge paw, his arm drawing back for the throw. Old-timers about the place had seen the flashing speed of his hurling, the deadly accuracy of a blade which could halve an apple at twenty feet. Even the calm of Marian's face dissolved in a scream—or at least her mouth was open, but no one heard the sound.

It was drowned in the sharper blast of a revolver, and Hartse stood for a moment, rocking on the balls of his feet, a stupid look of incomprehension washing across the wreck of his face. The knife clattered at his own feet, and then, knees buckling, he sank down to the floor with a lingering reluctance. Only as he reached it did a fresh red stain begin to show on his shirt front beside the huge diamond.

Straightening, still painfully sucking breath into empty lungs, Rawe North looked incredulously at the fallen man, then to the gun in Devero's hand. Tripp Devero was smiling, but there was strain behind it. His eyes roved the faces of those about him, and he checked the motion of breaking open the gun to punch out the empty shell.

12

"Time to get out of here—fast!" he hissed at North. "You too, Marian."

Her face, for an instant, had gone loose and child-like. Now it cleared and she grabbed North's arm and urged him toward the door. Devero was at their heels, his gun menacing the room. Even so, one of the men paid for this sort of job lunged behind the shelter of the bar and threw a quick shot. It smashed a hanging lamp in line with Devero's head, sending glass showering down in a reek of oil. He flung back a warning bullet, just above the heads of the panicky crowd, and ducked through the door behind the others.

Boots thudded loud on the plank sidewalk which here ran on two sides of the Paddle Wheel. The night was dark here in the street, the vagrant moon which had been overhead when Devero had entered the saloon now obscured by clouds. More boots pounded the planks from the other side, and he knew what was happening.

The hand which had paid their wages was limp, and no man who had taken Pete Hartse's pay had held any love for him. But they had drawn that pay and they were impelled now by a sense of loyalty, and if they would hold up their heads among others of their own ilk, they could do no less than kill those in turn who had been responsible for their employer's fall.

Which meant that they were losing no time. There was a door down at one side, a window on the other. They were using both of them to reach the two streets which flanked the main door, and from those points to converge upon it. The darkness helped, but that was a tenuous advantage at best. More roustabouts would debouch from behind, pocketing them in a three-way squeeze.

Marian Breen knew that as well as either of these men she fled with. They could fight, as had been demonstrated, but fighting against such odds would not be enough. She knew this building as they did not, and she acted swiftly, holding to North's arm with one hand, reaching with the other to catch at Devero.

"Here," she urged. "This way, quick!"

It was another door, close beside the main one, though few patrons of the saloon suspected its existence. No mere wood-butcher had hung it in place, but a carpenter who was also

13

an artisan. Outwardly there was no knob on it, no sign to indicate that there was a door or any break in the wall at all. But there was a way to open it, and the secret had long belonged to Marian. Inside was a narrow hallway, leading back to her own dressing room.

Not that this door had been built for the accommodation or convenience of herself or others like her who might work for Pete Hartse. Quite a contrary purpose had been in his mind when he devised it. A notion which she had driven well into the background of his thoughts when she had first been billed here as the Golden-Throated Thrush. For a long while now, secure bolts had closed this door on the inside, just as other bolts had closed the passageway off, where it reached her own dressing room.

But this evening, seeing these two men from the far reaches of the Arkansas out in front, she had acted on sudden impulse before going out to sing, had taken a quick moment to unlock the doors.

Now, inside the passage, she paused to bar the door. It was pitch black in here, and both men stood puzzled, apprehensive, unsure what to do. Then, her hands on their arms, she was guiding them again.

"Here," she instructed. "Wait a moment." She opened the door ahead, and they heard another bolt shoot home, then light came as she lit a lamp, adjusted the wick and put the glass chimney on. Only then did they see that it was her dressing room.

"We're safe enough for the present," she declared. "Listen!" And they could hear the confusion of the outer night, where those who had sought them searched, baffled, but convinced that somehow they had gotten away. She turned then to look at North, who was himself again.

"You were saying something when Hartse interrupted," she reminded him coolly.

North eyed her in frank admiration.

"I was sayin' that I aimed to have the biggest ranch and the best wife in Kansas," he said. "And I knew you'd see it my way, sweetheart. Ain't another woman to match you in all this stretch of country. Just as there's no other man to match me or ranch to match mine. We belong together."

Devero had been listening with a detached air. Now, coolly, he punched out the empty shells from his gun and inserted fresh ones, closing one eye in a slow wink as he did so.

"Conceited cuss, ain't he, Marian?" he grinned.

"Conceit?" North whirled on him. "You sided me, in there, Devero, which I ain't forgettin'—"

"We're both from the same place, both outlanders," Devero murmured. "Here we stand together against the crowd. That's all. It don't make us friends."

"That's what I was going to say," North growled. "I'd side you as quick, under the same circumstances. But it don't make us friends—ever. We're both too big, too close neighbors for that—even if it wasn't for the woman here. Sooner or later, I'll have to smash you."

"Or be smashed," Devero amended, and shoved the gun back in holster.

Marian eyed them curiously.

"In that case," she said, "I'd have thought you'd have stood aside."

"I would have, if he'd left the knife out of it," Devero agreed cheerfully. "But I never could abide knives."

"Enough of talk," North said harshly. "You told Hartse tonight that you were through here, Marian. That meant that you'd already decided to go with me."

"With one of you," she amended thoughtfully. "You both made big claims. But I've told both of you, before, that I'm for sale only to the highest bidder. Just what do you have on that ranch of yours, Rawe?"

"Plenty," North said confidently. "It's the biggest ranch in Kansas—bigger than you can ride over in three days. And it'll be bigger. I've fifteen thousand head of cattle runnin' on my range now, and I'll double that number. I've built the finest house in Kansas—that's what I've been doing since I met you here a year ago, girl. I doubt if there's a house in St. Louis, even, to match it."

Her eyes widened slightly, shifted to Devero, seated now on the edge of the dressing table. He was swinging one booted foot and whistling softly between his teeth.

"That's right, Marian," he agreed. "About the house. I've seen it. Makes my soddie look plumb like a gopher hole."

"Which is what it will be, when my herds run over it," North added harshly. "I've a third more range and twice as

15

many cattle as Tripp, and he's my biggest rival in Kansas. I've worked at more than buildin' a house this last year. I've doubled my graze, drove three trail herds up from Texas. Nobody is going to top my bid!"

Again she looked from one to the other, momentarily seeming a little uncertain of herself. Outside, the confusion had quieted. Devero still swung his spurred boot and whistled and smiled to himself as though amused by it all.

"We'll be married in the morning and start back right away," North added. "I've got a big wagon fitted up for your accommodation, and a wench to look after your wants along the way."

Marian nodded, but she shook her head as well.

"Not here, Rawe," she denied. "Not where I'm known. We'll be married after we reach your ranch."

North chuckled in high good humor.

"Aimin' to look it over first and make sure Tripp can't top my bid, eh?" he said. "Which suits me fine. You're the kind of a woman for a man like me to team with. We'll have such a wedding as Kansas has never seen!"

- 3 -

Sт. Louis by day was a town which Tripp Devero liked better by night. The dark at least hid some of its rough squalor, around such establishments as the Paddle Wheel, of which there were far too many for his taste. Maybe it was because he was accustomed to the wide reaching spaces of Kansas, of Texas and the lands in between. Country where a man had room in which to breathe. But in any case there had been only one attraction in St. Louis for him, and she was leaving it empty today.

He was saddling his own horse at a livery stable when the marshal came in. A tall man, past his years of flat leanness and unswerving sureness of mind and arm. His height now was muted by the bulge of a paunch, a flabbiness which extended to sagging jowls and mottled cheeks and shone out of reddened watery eyes. Here the law was past the hard incisiveness of the frontier, like the town itself. Unsure, and so inclined to bluster.

16

"You're Tripp Devero," the marshal accused. "From off on the Arkansas."

Devero nodded, pulling the cinch tight. He unhooked the stirrup from saddle horn and dropped it in place.

"You've got me tagged right," he conceded. "Fame sure travels a long way! Think of me bein' known here in the city!"

This levity did nothing to dissipate the marshal's sourness.

"I been lookin' for you," he said. "You shot Pete Hartse last night."

"I should of done it sooner, maybe," Devero sighed. "Only he didn't raw me too much the first time I saw him, and then I was out of town quite a spell till last night."

The marshal stared. Red flowed under his skin, making the mottled effect more toad-like.

"You braggin' about killin' a man?" he demanded.

Devero shook his head in shocked surprise.

"Course not," he said. "But I figgered you was here to express your thanks for me takin' the chore off your hands. Your town'll be that much a better place to live in now."

The marshal did not argue the point. But he persisted glumly.

"Why'd you have to kill him? I know how he was going to knife yore friend—but killin's pretty drastic."

"Whoa up there," Devero protested. "Rawe North's no friend of mine. On the other hand, I'd warned I'd see fair play. I don't often draw a gun, Marshal." He shook his head, added gravely, "But when I do, it's for keeps."

The marshal looked rather helplessly at him as he swung into the saddle, then stood uncertainly aside. Devero gave him an airy salute and rode out into the street. He pulled up, five minutes later, beside a covered wagon which waited with its team of heavy cayuses tied to a hitch-rail. They were true cayuse stock, he observed, but a couple of hundred pounds heavier per animal than the average cow pony. They'd snake that wagon across the prairie a third faster than an Eastern team could manage.

The wagon itself was new, the paint still gleaming, untouched by dust. A Peter Schutter wagon, built in Chicago, made with pioneer travel in mind. These things Devero noted mechanically, but his real attention was for Marian Breen,

17

on the seat of the wagon. A changed Marian from the Thrush of the Paddle Wheel. Gone was her finery of turkey red, replaced by a simple, serviceable traveling dress. But where she should have appeared more drab she shone instead. An inner glow, joyous, anticipatory. She was like a bird released from a cage, ready at long last to try its wings.

The wench, Judy, her face glistening with sweat, was tugging trunks and bags into new orderliness behind the seat. For the moment there was no sign of Rawe North.

Devero swept off his hat, his ready grin that of a carefree boy. He lounged in the saddle, appraising with eyes which, the girl felt, missed no details of what went on. His appearance of light-hearted ease, of careless indifference, was apt to be deceptive.

"I'm sure tickled to see that you're gettin' ready to head out for the big lands, Honeycake," he said. "Just ain't no place like the edge of things, with plenty of room beyond. How you could stand it cooped up here this long is hard to figure."

"A woman sometimes sees such things different than a man," Marian retorted. "But I don't think I'll ever understand you, Tripp. You say that you're pleased—when you know that I'm going out there to marry Rawe."

Devero's grin lost none of its amusement.

"That's what you *think* you're going out there for," he said. "Could be you're wrong. A calf's still a maverick till it gets a brand on its side and a slit in its ear. How many times a rider casts a loop its way don't count none till then."

She studied him, her dark eyes speculative, still puzzled.

"No, I don't think I'll ever understand you, Tripp," she repeated. "You're a strange man. . . . But when I give my word, I stick to it."

"And I sure wouldn't love you the way I do if you didn't," Devero retorted. "I'll dance at your wedding, don't worry. Right now, and though it breaks my heart, I'll have to be going on ahead of you. Got things to do, back at the Arkansas. Important ones. I just stopped to kiss you good-bye— for this time."

Before she suspected his intention, he had kneed his horse alongside the wagon, leaned suddenly across and kissed her on the mouth. For a moment sheer surprise held her frozen;

18

her lips were firm but with a yielding softness, sweet like wild strawberries.

Then red flamed across her face like the setting sun breaking through a cloud-bank. Her hand lashed out stingingly across his cheek, so that for a moment the finger-marks showed white and distinct, before flooding dark in their turn. But her voice was curiously breathless.

"You—you—what did you do that for?"

"Wanted to," Devero said matter-of-factly. "Liked it even better'n I thought I would, too."

He had been about to say more, blandly disregardful of her fury, but now Rawe North came up, the clatter of his horse's hoofs like pistol shots on the hard-packed street. His own face was red, and it was apparent that he had seen the whole thing. His voice was raw as his name.

"Damn you, Devero," he choked. "You go too far!"

"All the way to the Arkansas," Devero agreed blandly. "Be ridin' well ahead of you folks. Just stopped to kiss the bride. You don't know your luck, Rawe."

"You don't know yours," North returned coldly. "If it wasn't for last night, I'd kill you for what you did just now."

Devero had already swung his horse about, and it was tossing its head in a vast impatience to be gone. Now he pulled it back again, and there was no levity in his face or voice.

"I told you I was kissin' the bride," he reminded. "And, when I feel like it, I'll do it again!"

Brittleness was in the air, as though it could shatter at a touch, breaking those who breathed it. Devero caught a glimpse of Marian's face, of the appeal in her eyes, and abruptly his own softened to that old, challenging grin. He lifted his hand in easy salute, cantered down the street and out of sight.

Rawe North swung in the saddle to stare after him, and his face was bleak and uncompromising as he watched.

"One of these days," he said, "I'll have to kill him."

- 4 -

WEST, following near the line of steel whose twin rails North had adopted for his own brand. West, through a land grown old overnight, settled and sedate. Rawe North had ridden here when this, like the lands on the Arkansas now, was open far as the eye could reach, when buffalo were as likely to be encountered as the big trail herds up from Texas. When, aside from the cowboys who companied these herds, no human foot trespassed here or human eye scanned the empty horizon, save only the Indian.

That had not been long ago. He had been just a boy then, a boy doing a man's work, on his first long drive. It had not even entered his head that the immensity of this land could be changed, its emptiness filled in his own lifetime. There had been the big trail north at Independence, the road to Oregon. But what was one road in a limitless land?

The coming of the railroad had changed all that. Here were homesteads, changing already to settled farms, villages growing to towns and towns threatening to become cities. Plowed land and fenced fields, roads laid in a straight line instead of twisting where a man's fancy might lead him. He was like Tripp Devero in one way. This was a nightmare.

But Rawe North was unlike Devero in the motivating reason. Whereas Devero loved the open because it was wild and free, North had more practical reasons. There was land out there on the far reaches of the Arkansas—free land for the taking, to the man big enough in vision, strong enough to grasp and hold it. An empire, where a man might reign as a king. Land and cattle meant wealth and power, and North was greedy for both.

There was a lesson here for men such as he, and looking about on the smokes which arose from a thousand scattered soddies or new-built frame houses, he took it to heart. This had been a cattle empire a few short years ago, its sod unbroken save by the goring horns or trampling hoofs of the buffalo since the polar ice cap had relinquished its arctic clutch in a forgotten past. Free land and open, but claimed now by a new breed of men as alien to the cattlemen as they in turn had been to the Indian.

This had taken them unaware, this march of the homesteader—men who had swarmed like the grasshoppers, as persistent and as devouring. They had won, the little men. But with this lesson before him, he would see to it that such were turned back when they reached the edge of his dominion. When landgrabbers got that far, he would be ready for them.

His Rail Road Track spread was as far from the actual railroad as he could well get in these days. That absence of steel was a boon to the big landholder, though a railroad within driving distance was a key to prosperity because it insured a market for his beef. But prosperity had been followed too often by the curse of those who came behind the rails.

He had traveled to unsurveyed land, free as this had been a few years before. He had taken it as other cattlemen had taken land before him. The difference would be that he would hold what he claimed—hold it against all comers.

North turned now to glance toward the wagon, to where Marian rode. She had raised no objection to the slower journey west by wagon. Time could have been saved by going a good part of the way by train. But, like Tripp Devero who had ridden ahead, North hated the train. He had traveled this country by horse and wagon when there was no other way to go, and it was still the natural thing to him. Besides, with such company, he was in no hurry.

An interlude such as this was pleasant, a pause from fighting. For that was what his life had been, almost as far back as he could remember—a continual struggle, a constant fight for survival and for mastery. It attested to his ability that he had not only survived in a rough land but had mastered wherever he went. His name, as he had always felt, was prophetic. And he had worked to make it so.

Rawe North. It was the right name for him. The Norths had always been strong, ruthless men, like the land the name suggested. His mother had been a Rawe of Kentucky, and that in itself told all that most people needed to know. So now he was a man for his environment, and he had found a woman to match him.

He swung closer alongside the wagon, observing pridefully how effortlessly Marian Breen controlled the fractious team.

21

Like himself, she could handle horses or men. And like himself, she knew exactly what she wanted, and no price was too high to pay to get it. Conversely, nothing short of her goal would satisfy her. Again like him, she was not one to be swayed by foolish sentiment. In that, she was a woman in a million. The one woman he had ever found to measure up to his own harsh standard.

"This was open land, ten years ago," he observed. "Not a house in a hundred miles. Country like the Arkansas is now. Only out there it's going to stay that way!"

"Do you think you can keep it so?" she asked.

"I'll hold what I take," he promised. "There's one law on the frontier—the law of the gun. I've never seen the man could beat me that way."

"How about Devero?" Marian asked. "I hear he's never been bested."

North's smile was grim.

"A man's never bested but once, that way," he retorted. "It's true, he's probably the best man there is across a thousand miles—next to me. He's a man I could like—if he hadn't made two mistakes."

"And those?" she asked.

"Pitchin' his spread next to mine, for one thing. There's a lot of room out there, but not enough for the two of us. And wantin' the same woman. I might pass up the one—but not the other."

She surveyed him, this man she had agreed to marry, with eyes faintly troubled. Troubled but not disillusioned. She had foreseen with sure clarity what the outcome of this clash must be. One would survive. Only one.

Where a lesser woman would have shrunk from the issue she had faced it. She was the issue, and she knew it. Both wanted her, and both were strong men in a ruthless land. If the issue were not fought on the Arkansas it would be settled in St. Louis, and whether she liked it or not. It was not in the nature of either of them to consult her about their own differences.

That was what she liked about them. She might have settled it in a third way by marrying some other man. But after seeing these two, she knew that she could never be content with one of the lesser breed. There was destiny out ahead, there on the winding banks of the Arkansas. Destiny beyond Wichita.

Remembering the quick, hard pressure of a mouth against her own, gay laughing eyes and the gun-swift speed which had beaten the knife in the hand of Hartse, she felt a strange stirring in her like sap rising in the red willows at springtime. She had made her choice with her head, but sometimes, deep down, she was still a woman with a woman's unruly heart.

- 5 -

THEY HAD LEFT the old lands behind. Those settled fields, grown old in a night, tamed and harnessed, where even the wind, sweeping hard behind the rain, seemed no longer quite the same. Wichita was behind them, and the still-pushing line of steel, its raw snout burrowing like a mole across the land, scarring as it shoved, was turned away from them.

Here was the new land, old and unchanged since time had smiled upon it and the prisoning ice had withdrawn. Old but new, the newness of the untamed frontier. Again Rawe North swung his horse alongside the jouncing wagon.

"Another three days," he pronounced, "and we'll be there. I hope you'll like it, Marian. I've built the biggest house this side of St. Louis for you. Twelve rooms, and big ones. Frame, with windows and hardware, all freighted out from the railroad. I had to order some of the furniture from New York and Philadelphia. I've had twenty men working on the house for a half year, and as many more planting a lawn and bringing in trees and fixing the grounds. I hope you'll like it."

She looked at him steadily for a moment, seeing him as he would never see himself—a strong man, rough-edged, harsh and unlovely of exterior. Perhaps as hard within, since here a man must be hard if he would survive, to say nothing of dominating. And she had chosen him because he could dominate, and in doing that, offer her what she wanted.

Yet this was a side hidden from most people, a part of him generally unsuspected. A softening, redeeming trait which she had guessed at before.

Despite that deep-buried part of him, he had spoken no

23

word of love. She doubted if he ever would. This was a business proposition with him, as he had made sure that it was with her. She would grace his empire, a queen at the heart of it, throned in the big house. She would be the mother of strong sons in the tradition of the Rawes and the Norths. Both of them were getting what they wanted, and neither, as he saw it, would have cause to repent of their bargain.

That was all that he saw or knew of himself. But he had built this house for her. Partly as a bribe, a part of the price which she would exact for leaving St. Louis and coming to a raw land. Partly as a sop to his own pride of achievement. All of that she recognized. But he had built it in part, she liked to believe, for her—the woman. That it might say to her what he would never find the words to voice.

"I'll like it, Rawe," she agreed. "Don't let that worry you."

"I'm not worried," he denied. "I've found that I can get what I want by going after it. So I don't worry."

In that, far more simply than he knew, was expressed the philosophy of the man. A strange restlessness, a growing eagerness, was in him. It lay in part, he supposed, in returning home again. And a part would be in the imminence of his marriage to this woman, which would mark a definite milestone in his life, an accomplishment to rate with the claiming of this land, the overflowing of it with cattle bearing his brand, or the building of his big house. Conquest!

But the last weeks, save for that single episode in St. Louis, that fight with Hartse, had been tame ones and uneventful. He tingled for action, for a good fight. And there would be a fight ahead. Of that he had not the least doubt. He and Tripp Devero had an issue to settle between them—

A speck had appeared upon the horizon, growing in size with a long tail behind. A tail of dust, hanging like a haze in the air. There had been no rain since leaving the Missouri country. Dust rolled with the wagon, rose up in little pops from every fall of the horses' hoofs. The grass was luxuriant, but it was cured and brown. The blue haze of late summer was in the air, shimmering on the horizon.

Now the rider was close enough for North to recognize him. A dark man, product of Basque and Louisiana French —a hot blood of long mixing in hot lands by the river, come now to a strong potency in Noland Doll. He was like the low-slung gun he wore, a fancy gun with silver filigree, but deadly. He was Rawe North's right-hand man, and no one ever made fun of his name—at least not a second time.

Seeing the way he rode, North swore, deep in his throat, and put his own horse to a run. He met Doll a mile from the wagon, and read the trouble in his face.

"What's wrong?" he demanded. No word of greeting, after these long weeks. But Doll was not the man for frills.

"There's hell to pay," Noland Doll said shortly. "I've been ridin' all night and the day. You got a fresh horse for me? This one's near finished."

"There's an extra one back at the wagon," North agreed.

"Then I'll take it. We'd better be gettin' back so you can take a hand, fast."

North's lips compressed. But he asked no further questions as they rode, more slowly, back toward the oncoming wagon. Here was trouble already, for Doll was not the man to exaggerate. He voiced a name.

"Devero?"

"Yeah," Doll said thinly.

North eyed him bleakly. The same stirring impatience was in him now that Doll was voicing, but he had long since learned to look after his men. Doll had ridden his horse almost to death, had driven himself in the same relentless fashion.

"Want to eat and rest a while?"

Doll shook his head.

"Not now. Time enough for that."

North introduced him briefly as they reached the wagon. Already, save for one searching glance at this woman whom his employer had ridden to St. Louis to fetch, Noland Doll was untying the fresh cayuse behind the wagon, replacing it with his own. Stripping off the saddle and slapping it on the fresh horse with a driving impatience.

"There's trouble at the ranch," North told Marian. "I've got to get there now. You'll be all right. There's nothing along the road these days to bother you. Just follow the track three days, and you'll be there."

"Of course," Marian agreed. "I'll be fine." She waited, expecting some farewell, planning then to tell him that she

25

hoped the trouble would not be too great. But Doll had the saddle on now. He jerked the stirrup off the saddle-horn, stuck his toe in and was up as the cayuse was away at a run. Rawe North lifted his hand in brief salute and was beside him, and the dust ran in a long wave behind them.

- 6 -

NOLAND DOLL was a tight-twisted man, made darker by sun and wind. A man hard and tough as the saddle he rode in. A man who had literally cut his teeth on a gun barrel and been inured to hardship on the long drives up from Texas. He rode past the going down of the sun with no sign of checking, onward through the closing night as fast as horses could maintain the pace, in silence.

North raised no objection, offered no suggestion, and asked no further question. By streaks Doll was a garrulous man. It bespoke the gravity of the situation that he rode now with clamped jaw. But finally, as North had known he must, he spoke.

"I was off on the Little Cottonwood when it happened," he said, as though the words were dragged from him. "Toby Miller had been shot over there, and I figured I'd better see about it. I should have stayed at home."

Rawe North was a hard man, but he was fair.

"You couldn't tell that," he said.

"Maybe it's why I'm alive to tell you now," Doll muttered, and rage thickened his tones. "Though I might have killed a few of them first!"

"Devero's men?"

"Maybe. I wasn't thinkin' so much of them. It's our own crew—most of the yellow skunks sold out. Took his pay. That's why the few that stayed loyal didn't have a chance."

"You mean—I've no crew left?"

"No crew, no cattle—no nothin'," Doll said savagely, and relapsed into silence again.

North did not question him. He was staggered, but he had heard enough. Bleakness was in him, like the chill in the wind which stirred now across the hidden land. A bleak bitterness which rose up hot and ugly in his mouth, that numbed his

26

brain even as it made it more alive. Here was trouble, as he had known there would be. Trouble, and a fight ahead.

It was more than that. For the moment he refused to think how much more it might be. Never did he allow himself to worry. As he had told Marian, he had always been able to get what he wanted by going after it. There might be delays, defeats, setbacks. But in the long run he triumphed. He always had. It was certain in his own mind that he always would.

Even so, it came as a shock to him when daylight pushed aside the cloak as they reached his own empire. The grass had been green when he had ridden away, rains washing across the land, freshening it. Vast herds of cattle, all wearing the Rail Road Track on their left ribs, all with four ears, as it appeared, from the Jingle Bob which, like John Chisum in Texas and New Mexico, North had adopted for his own sign here in Kansas. These herds, his herds, watched by his crews, had spread across the land. And his big house, two stories high, with great pillars in the front of it, patterned after the mansions of the Old South, shining in its first coat of white paint, had been nearing completion.

Time had brought change. Change which made him suck in his breath painfully. Here at his feet his horse still stood in good brown grass, cured dry by the sun. But this was the edge of the grass, the beginning of devastation. No longer did greenery spread like a living carpet between and beyond the two horizons. Here was emptiness, a black scar upon a tortured earth.

Far as he could see was the bare black ground with no spear of grass remaining. Fire had swept here, only a few days before. The smell of it, like a sickness, came up at him in a wave, causing the horses to paw and nicker anxiously. But the ground was cold and no smoke arose. There was no living thing, cattle or horse or man as far as the eye could reach.

"How long ago?" he asked tightly.

"I saw the smoke as I headed back from the Cottonwood," Doll said wearily. "A shower came up—the first in weeks. Too late to do any good. But it put it out."

There was no sign of the rain left now in the parched, thirsty ground. There would be more rains soon, as the clouds

27

in the east promised this morning. But they, too, would be too late.

"How far?"

"Almost all the range."

"And the herd?"

"They were driven off first—our own crew helpin'."

"And the house?"

It lay beyond the horizon, but already he knew the answer. Doll's voice added confirmation.

"One buildin' still stands—the old cook house. That's all."

It was characteristic of North that he asked no more questions. For a few minutes he sat, erect in the saddle, staring out at this desolation which represented the blasting of his hopes. Here was ruin, stark and complete. But he did not bother with details.

Men had been killed. He knew that, but dead men, even though they might have died loyally in his service, were of no further use to him. Other men had been hired away, had turned traitor. One day he would settle with them, but for the time being there was no need to know their names. Time enough for that when he was in a position to watch them die.

It was long miles across the burned strip to where one building still stood. There would be water there, but he had no desire to see the ashes of his big house. Traveling to it would waste the better part of a day, and serve no useful purpose.

Looking south, he could see the line of black stretching to the horizon. Better to ride where the grass still ran. Down beyond the horizon he could obtain food and fresh horses. Far enough to the south lay Texas.

Already his mind was shaping a plan, coldly, methodically. It would be folly to search for herds missing for days, with no crew behind him. Worse folly to hunt out Tripp Devero for settlement without men to back his play. All of those matters would have to be postponed.

"We're startin' for Texas," he informed Doll. "Did the fire hit Prescott's?"

"I hear it missed him."

"We'll reach there by noon. Fresh horses. Supplies. And sleep the clock round. I'll get money when we need it. We'll reach Texas and get a new crew—a big one. And some new

28

herds. What's sauce for Kansas I'll stir to gravy in Texas. The grass'll be green here, time we get back with new herds."

Doll eyed his employer with something close to hero worship in his eyes. It was this cold-blooded way of planning far ahead, of executing emotionlessly, that had tied his destiny to North's. Here was ruin, but it was not feazing North for a moment. Exactly what his plan might be Doll did not know, but he knew that North had one already. He could almost envision their return with a force so overwhelming that nothing could check them. Settlement would be delayed, but no longer than the time required to make it a grim and final accounting.

"But what about—her?" Doll asked. "She'll be comin' along in a day or two. I—thought you aimed to get married—"

"She's able to look after herself," North retorted. "I can't waste three days—and there's nothing to wait for—now."

Doll looked at him as he turned his horse's head. He wanted to ask another question, but he knew better than to voice it. *What of Devero? He's the big man now. What of Devero—and her, if you leave her alone?* For Doll had heard the talk that this woman was interested in a man not for what he was but for what he possessed. And that her favor had hinged narrowly between the two big men of the Arkansas.

North seemed to sense the unspoken question. He voiced grim answer to it.

"Whatever happens," he said, "I get what I want—sooner or later. And I'll kill Tripp Devero—sooner or later."

- 7 -

TIGHTNESS had been building up in Marian Breen for the past couple of days. Her pride had been that she knew what she wanted, and that nothing would be allowed to stand in the way of getting it. A pride of self-sufficiency in any situation.

But this vast reaching land, limitless as time, lonely as space, was disconcerting. She was accustomed to St. Louis, to crowds. Here there was only the wagon, the horses, her maid and herself. Even the occasional cowboys, the grazing herds, the wild animal life which had been common up to a few days ago, had disappeared. Now there were only the two horizons, which came no nearer, though you traveled forever toward the one ahead.

North had not returned. She had not expected it of him. But when the wagon came at last to the edge of the burned land she knew dismay. Here was something elemental, gigantic. And catastrophic. The immensity of it became more apparent as she drove forward, following the road, still visible through the burned.

Somewhere out here wound the Arkansas River. She had dreamed of a green and fruitful land, of a welcome as a bride. Here was emptiness and worse. The wench had whimpered in terror, imploring her to go no farther. But she had set her course, and there could be no turning back. Only now a new fear was in her heart. That Tripp Devero had done this. . . .

The immensity of desolation closed around them. Some miles deep in it were grim reminders of what the holocaust had been, flames racing madly in sun-cured grass, driven by the wind. They came upon occasional scattered bodies—of rabbits, as she guessed, of other creatures somewhat larger. It was hard to tell, blackened and discolored, swollen as they were, their decay a drifting stench on the wind.

Those victims had possessed an instinct to flee, had been for the most part fleet of foot, tireless in endurance. They should have been able to outrun even prairie fire. Unless— and the thought bulked monstrous in her mind—unless this blaze had been started at many points at once, over a wide area. The very position of these charred remains, along a narrow strip or so, as if driven and caught between two fires, seemed to indicate that such had been the case.

Nowhere was there grass on which a cow might graze. Nor sign of any of the herds of which Rawe North had boasted.

Some of the fear which beset her companion was like a numbness in her own heart, so that she was almost ready to turn the team, when finally she glimpsed the river in the distance. In this blackness it was like a river of life flowing out of Eden, into the wilderness. .

The simile was all but gone when finally she reached it, still following the old wagon trail. The river ran clear and

30

sweet, but the blackness was on both sides of it. Here was a little valley with low hills. Blackened stumps of trees remained, pointing like stark accusing fingers. Then, topping a rise, she pulled the team up and drew in her breath with a shudder.

Even without the mute reminders she would have known that this was the place. Whether by chance or by skill, North had chosen well in picking his homesite. A quarter of a mile back from the river, cupped by these little hills, she could see, even now, that it must have been a place of natural beauty. A small stream wound down from the north and hurried to meet the river. The giant, charred trunk of a cottonwood still stood, and its higher branches held green leaves, twisted and curled but not consumed.

There were deeper piles of ashes where big buildings had stood—she could tell where a barn had been, a corral, on both sides of the creek, the mansion which North had built for her. The still raw grounds about it made its location certain.

What brought the gasp to her throat was the certainty that no grass fire had been responsible for the carnage here. North had prudently been on guard against such a happening. A big fire-guard had been plowed all around, and the prairie blaze had advanced that far and no farther. Because of the building, the new landscaping and the trampled ground around barn and corrals, there had been still more protection, where no fire could find fuel to run. The signs indicated clearly that the buildings had been deliberately fired.

Final proof was that one still stood. A stout log structure, squat and unlovely. As she looked toward it, one hand went suddenly to her mouth to choke back a scream.

The door of this house stood open, looking dark and lonely. But a figure had suddenly appeared in it, coming slowly out into the sun. A creature so dreadful of aspect that for a moment even the tired horses raised their heads and snorted.

Then quick sympathy replaced the first emotion, and Marian climbed swiftly down over the wagon wheel. It was a man who stood there, pitiful and uncertain. His clothes were torn and with evidences of the flames about them, he was hatless and a part of his hair had been singed away, as well as eyebrows and lashes. He stood, hands outstretched

31

gropingly, and then he took a step and stumbled and fell headlong.

His face was worst. The flame which had scorched his hair had blistered it, so that it was swollen and discolored. As she neared him, Marian saw that his eyes were closed, but mattered and repulsive. Whiskers straggled unevenly in this blotched mask.

"What happened?" Marian cried, and saw how he shrank and cringed, as if from a blow. Her voice grew gentle.

"Don't be afraid. We're friends. We're going to help you."

"A—a woman?" he said uncertainly, and managed, clumsily, to sit up on the ground. "I—I thought I heard somebody comin'. If—if I could have a drink—"

"Of course," Marian agreed, and called the maid, just getting timidly down from the wagon. "Judy, take a bucket and get some water. Hurry, now!"

The man drank thirstily and seemed relieved. His voice was apologetic.

"I—I couldn't seem to find the creek," he explained. "There was a bucket of water in the house, but when that was gone—I just ain't much good, seems like."

"What happened to you?" Marian asked. "Your face—"

"I kind of took a charge of shot in my face," he said. "And then I couldn't see—"

Gradually she got the story from him. How raiders had swept down just at dawn, without warning. There had been a battle, short and sharp, that much he knew. But he had been struck in the face with a charge of bird-shot from a shotgun almost at the first, and had been blinded and helpless. He didn't think that the shot had been fired at him. He had just happened to be in the wrong place at the wrong time.

Beyond that he knew little. Aware that carnage was going on all around him, blinded and in agony, he had stumbled about and crouched in the edge of the creek. If anyone had seen him, no one had paid much attention to him. Silence had descended as abruptly as the disturbance had begun, and he had walked uncertainly, hearing the crackle of flames. Once he had almost been caught between two fires, and had suffered the burns. But finally it had all been over with, and he had come upon the old cook house, still standing. It had been somewhat apart from the others.

32

"Who—do you know who did this?" Marian asked.

"I couldn't see 'em," he said apologetically. "But I did hear some of 'em talking. They said their boss, Tripp Devero, 'd be plumb pleased with the job they were doing."

Tripp Devero! The ice that had been in her veins seemed to be congealing in her heart. But that was merely confirmation of what she had been fearing, believing, ever since coming to the edge of the black lands. Tripp Devero!

But why should she be surprised? She had known his reputation. She had seen him kill a man as quickly and as coolly as he would a chicken. She had known that there would be war, here on the Arkansas—

But such a war as this! It drew a shuddering breath from her, and then she was herself again, knowing the needs of this derelict of a man.

"Get a fire going in that stove inside," she ordered Judy. Heat some water. And find something to cook. He's starving."

For the next hour she forced herself, with a stern calmness, to a task which sent revulsion all through her. Always she had been dainty to a point which her companions considered ridiculous in a frontier town. She shrank from even casual physical contact with most people, and sickness or disease appalled her. She was no one to nurse the ill, she had always believed.

But this was a job which had to be done, and she did not neglect it. Assisted by Judy, they washed and cleaned the ravaged face and chest, shoulders and arms, as well as they could. Flinching from the task more than the patient, she picked out many of the shots which were festering in such ugly fashion, and applied grease to the burns.

It was not too bad—aside from his eyes. There was not much to be done for them, but she feared that his sight was gone. He needed a doctor, and there was no doctor. He was grateful for help, and endured the painful ordeal stoically. To divert him as much as possible she talked while she worked, learning that he had been one of the cowboys here. His name was Farris, Bud Farris. And he had been alone here since disaster had struck.

He had seen no sign of Rawe North, not for many long weeks. No one, he was sure, had been here since the fire.

"Law me, Miss Marian, we best be gittin' back out o'

here," Judy protested. "No tellin' where Mistah Nawth gone to now. Mebby he been kilt, too. This is a plumb heathenish country. Sooner we get back to wheah folks is people, sooner I gwine breathe again. An' besides, this man need a doctah."

"He's been nearly a week without one, and it would take another week at least to reach help," Marian pointed out. "Right now what he needs is rest and plenty of food—and there's enough of that for a few days," she added, having made a survey inside the house. "Mr. North will be back as soon as he can manage, of course. We'll wait."

It was the only thing to do, she assured herself. A new emotion touched her at thought of North, akin to pity. He had worked hard, had built up his spread and his hopes, only to return to this. The treachery and ruthlessness of the attack filled her with horror. But Rawe North was not the man to submit tamely. He was out to retaliate—to recover his stolen herds if he could. Perhaps, even now, he would be facing Tripp Devero in a show-down battle.

There was no comfort in that thought, and she shied from it. But he would remember her—he was to marry her. There was nothing to do but wait.

Under the influence of food and good care, Bud Farris made a good recovery. Save for his eyes, which still festered and were now kept bandaged, his face was doing well. Had it not been for his patient cheerfulness in the face of adversity, Marian doubted if she could stand it. The black emptiness of this land, the loneliness as the days passed, filled her with increasing dismay. Where was North?

It rained, beginning in the night. The drip of it was soothing, while the dark lasted. By day it grew monotonous, and it was worse to be penned in this small building. All that next night it rained, but by morning the sun shone again, and the land had a washed look. She stared, incredulous, then with understanding. The land was taking on a faint tinge of greenery as the grass started again.

That day she explored, gaining zest in the rain-fresh air, until she came upon four new, raw mounds at some distance from the buildings. So the invaders had taken time, at least, to bury their victims! But she was more depressed than ever as she returned to the house.

They had been here nearly a week now. The problem of

what to eat for man and beast alike was growing pressing. The grass was making the black earth green again, hiding the vast ugly scar of it, but she and Judy had been compelled to seek out small unburned patches which had been too green to be swept by the fire, close to the river, for the horses. Those were nearly gone now.

The horses would soon find grass, but their own larder was getting dangerously low. Why didn't North return? Was it because he was dead—

She shook such thoughts from her, fighting against panic. He *must* come soon. She pinned her faith to that. If he was pursuing his stolen herds, it would take time. He had said that it required three days to ride across his own land, and she no longer doubted it, knowing the vastness of these prairies.

Each day Judy guided Farris on a lengthening walk. They were out somewhere now, off by the river, trying to find more grass for the horses. Judy, at least, was walking. Bud Farris, being a cowboy, preferred to ride. The cayuses had not objected too strongly. Judy had stoutly declined the suggestion that she could ride as well. To Farris' protest that he had them gentled like kittens, she had shaken her head.

"I seen kittens hump they backs and spit an' claw—and I seen them horses do the same with you on 'em," she retorted. "No, suh, I got good legs. I walk."

That was what she should be doing, too—just for exercise, to fight the apathy, the curtain of fear which seemed to be closing about her. Fresh air and sun would be good for her. Marian knew it, but she sat in the house and could not bring herself to stir. If only North would come—

She heard it, then—the jingle of bridle bits, the quick, purposeful tinkle of spurred boots striding up to the door, and came to her feet, breathless and flushed. She'd known he would come—

The door opened, and she started forward, checked in dismay. It was Tripp Devero who stood there, grinning at her.

35

HE STARED for a moment, then swept off his hat. The same old Tripp, unabashed, just as he had been when she had seen him last, that morning in St. Louis—when he had ridden away after kissing her—

She felt the blood pounding in her cheeks at the remembrance, and at the tantalizing quality in his grin she knew that he remembered it too. Her fury mounted.

"You!" she breathed. "What are you doing here?"

"Why, I just dropped in to pay a neighborly call, honeycake," he protested. "Ain't you glad to see me?"

She was, now that the surprise of his arrival was past. Sight of any familiar face was welcome, after the long loneliness. But she would not admit as much to him.

"I'd sooner see the devil himself!" she flashed. "Or isn't there any difference?"

"Well, now—" Devero seemed to consider the question. "Maybe it's a lot in the way you look at it. Some folks don't like me, and that's a fact. Though I was hopin' you wasn't one of them."

"Why shouldn't I hate you?" Marian demanded. "After what you've done—murdering, stealing everything loose, burning and looting like a thief in the night, while Rawe was away."

For just a flickering instant it seemed to her that there was surprise, even bewilderment, in that devil-may-care face. But it was as quickly gone, so that in the next moment she doubted that she had seen it at all. His aggravating grin was back again.

"Well, now, ain't that the way to do things?" he drawled. "Take what you can get when you can get it? Special when it's a case of do it first or have it done to you?"

"I knew you were a killer, Tripp Devero! But I didn't think you were a sneaking coward to boot! Though I suppose I should have known. They go together, don't they?"

"My, but you're plumb cantankerous, ain't you, honeycake?" Devero drawled. "The Golden-Throated Thrush! I bet you ain't opened that pretty mouth of yours to warble in a long spell, now have you?"

His words startled her. Thinking back, she realized that she had not sung once, even to herself, since that last night in the Paddle Wheel.

"My singing is my business," she retorted coldly.

"And you get paid good money for it, or you don't peep," Devero mocked. "And out here there's no one to pay, of course. Now me, I ain't got much of a voice, as such go—though the cows don't object too much to my tries at a tune. Sometimes they even beller along with me. But mostly, I like to sing even if there ain't nobody or nothin' to hear, just for my own enjoyment. I'd rather hear you sing, any day, of course. Always seems to me that when a person does some carolin', it kind of keeps you from gettin' to hate yourself too much."

She knew what he meant. Out alone this way, it would help—and she had not even thought about it. Certainly she hadn't felt in the mood for singing these last several days. She lifted a disdainful shoulder at him, and he grinned again, his quick eyes moving appraisingly around the room.

"Heard it said, just yesterday, that Rawe is headin' south for Texas," Devero drawled. "Tom MacGorda met him and his foreman, Doll, days ago. They was far down the trail then, and burnin' daylight, not to mention bustin' horse-flesh."

Marian drew in her breath sharply. For a moment the news was stunning, incomprehensible, yet she could not doubt it. Nothing else would explain his failure to return. And at no time had she been able to bring herself to believe that he might be dead.

Devero did not elaborate, nor ask questions in turn. It was as though he had dropped an idle remark about one who was a mutual acquaintance, and expected no comment. But she knew that he guessed at the truth—that North had ridden away and left her, and that they had not been married. They could not have been, under the circumstances. If he had stopped to think much about her or her welfare, he would not have left her here, in this burned-over land, to subsist in a bare cabin. The depletion of all supplies would not have missed those searching eyes of Devero's.

There was nothing that she could say by way of denial,

and she knew it. Bewilderment was in her, coupled with hurt, and then a slow understanding began to come.

Rawe North was a practical man. He had wasted no time in whistling against the wind, in idle recrimination or in feeling sorry for himself, as lesser men would have done. His range was destroyed, but it would grow again. His herds were gone, and his crew with them. But there were vast herds in Texas, cheap cattle available almost for the taking. And men. Texans of a tough, fighting stock. It needed only a second thought for her to understand why North had not wasted an hour in heading for the Lone Star.

So far as she was concerned, she understood that too now, with bitter clarity. She had made it plain to him that she was not moved by emotion, that she was not for sale cheaply. He had known, without possibility of doubt, that she was accepting him because he had made the highest bid.

So he had been certain that, coming to the edge of the burned ground, seeing the devastation, knowing that he was ruined and would have nothing to offer her now, she would promptly turn back. The notion that there might be some womanliness deep down in her, a core of loyalty to him in his time of trouble, of faith to her own word, had never occurred to him at all.

What he planned to do was to recoup his fortunes and then return for her! Purely a matter of buying and selling, as he would do with a cow. Her cheeks flamed again.

"You're mighty purty, honeycake, when you color up that way," Devero drawled. "Fact is, you're the finest lookin' gal I ever set eyes on, anywhere, any time—or mebby I've told you that before!"

She faced him, her eyes stormy.

"Do you think it's fair or chivalrous to say such things to me, when you know that I'm going to marry another man?" she demanded. "But I suppose it's useless to mention such scruples to you. You like to take advantage of a man when he's away and can't help himself."

His eyes were sharp on her for a moment before that half mocking humor veiled them again.

"Now there's a thought!" he commented. "Somebody said a bunch of words once about makin' hay when the sun comes bright! But I always been too easy-going, lettin' too many chances slip. Thanks for pointin' out my opportunity."

"You're welcome for nothing," she retorted. "And now will you go?"

"Is that neighborly?" he chided. "And after me ridin' way over here? It ain't quite the same as crossin' a street in St. Louis. I been in the saddle since early yesterday, just to pay this call." He sighed elaborately. "Sure seems strange to see the Thrush in such surrroundings as this."

"It's due to a neighborly gesture with a match that I can't invite you into the big house which had been built," she reminded him bitingly.

"Golly now, this neighbor business stretches wide, don't it?" he sighed. "A plumb wide loop."

They had both remained standing—partly because there was only the single chair in the room, which she had been occupying before his arrival. Partly because she was of no mind to invite him to linger, even though she knew the rule of Western hospitality. There were a couple of stools, the edges of bunks along one wall.

Calmly he backed against the opposite wall, raising one spurred boot to rest against it. His glance was quizzical.

"I had a talk with you, Marian, back soon after I'd first met you," he reminded, with an abrupt change of manner. "You told me then that you'd been one of a big family, and never had had quite enough to eat or wear or keep warm by till you were fourteen. That because of that, you'd had enough of poverty, and knew just what you wanted—and intended to get it. Remember?"

"Of course I remember." She stood behind the chair now, hands resting on the back of it. "I haven't changed my mind."

"I was just wonderin'. You made a lot of things plain—or you sure used plain words. You weren't going to be ruled by sentiment, or emotion—nothing like that. When you found a man that had what you wanted, plenty of money—or land and cattle that would bring money—a man that could give you what you aimed to have out of life, you'd marry him. Not any other. That sounded so convincin' that I hypered home to kind of build up my spread. Then I went back to St. Louis, but seemed like I'd come a mite late. Like you'd had your bid matched."

She was silent, and he gestured with one hand.

"Whatever you expected, this is what you found. I didn't give up hope—not back at St. Louis. I figured somethin' might turn up—"

"And rode ahead to make sure that it did!"

"If I could," he acknowledged. "When you put the price high, a man has to meet it. What I'm drivin' at is this. North didn't have it to pay. Right now, I do—and I'm here, and so are you. You've known a long time that you're the only woman for me, Marian. Well—I got a big spread. A good many thousand head of cattle on it. My house isn't much, though it's a considerable improvement on this. And I'll build you a big one—as fine as you want."

For a moment he was quiet, serious. Then that tantalizing grin came out again.

"Ought to be an improvement, anyway. Course, I go with the deal. But you could do worse. If you'd like to do what you didn't do before, check to see how big the place is, count the cattle, why, I can show them to you—"

"Oh, stop!" she cried frantically. "Will you get out now—do you think I'm that sort of a woman?"

He eyed her uncertainly for a moment, and there was a new light in his eyes which surprised and startled her. Only for a moment and then it was gone, with that twisted, half mocking grin in its place.

"Anybody that thinks he knows a woman," he commented, " is sure a fool. And I reckon that goes for you as well as for any other female of the species."

"Since you've arrived at that weighty conclusion, will you get out?" she demanded again. "That's little enough that I ask, isn't it?"

Devero lowered his leg, only to elevate the other in turn against the wall. He shook his head, making no move to obey her request.

"Nope," he denied. "That's asking a whale of a lot. You'd ought to know that. Still, if it's what you want, why, I reckon you know well enough that I been your slave, grovelin' at your feet ever since I first set eyes on you."

"You appear to grovel!" she flashed.

"Don't I do a good job of it, though?" he echoed admiringly. "Yep, I sure enough do. So if you ask me to go—why,

40

I guess I might at that. Only first, honeycake. I want another kiss. I sure liked the taste of that other one. Been savorin' it for weeks now, lookin' forward to the next one."

"There'll be no next one!" she cried, and near panic was in her tones, to her own acute bewilderment. Secretly she raged, knowing that she too had remembered that other kiss —savored was the word he had used. Not for the world would she admit to anything like that, but the very notion upset her more than she would have believed possible.

"If you're a—a gentleman at all, get!" She added, almost imploringly, "Please go!"

He had lowered both feet to the floor now; his grin was like that of a coyote approaching a hen-yard.

"I'm no gentleman," he retorted. "I'm a devil—on plumb good authority. A feller that'll steal when he gets the chance. So I'm going to have another kiss if I have to steal it. Though if you'd prefer just to give it—"

She was backing away as he slowly advanced, still holding to the chair, dragging it with her, keeping it between them. There was wildness in her eyes now, a high color in her cheeks. Never had he seen her look so beautiful, even when artfully made up and sumptuously dressed for her part as the Thrush.

"I—I'll kill you," she warned desperately. "If you don't stop—"

His grin widened.

"I really believe maybe you would—if you had the chance," he agreed. "You're like me, I guess—got some of the devil in you, too. When you look at a man that way, you got to expect that he'll want a kiss. And when you call him all those names, don't you expect him to live up to 'em? Come on now, honeycake—one kiss, and my word on it that I'll do as you ask then—even to kissin' you twice if you want me to, or ridin' away with just the one, if you insist, though I sure won't want to!"

She was almost back to the other wall now, her ears strained for some sound which would indicate that Judy and Farris might be returning. But there was no sound at all, and she knew there would be none—not in time. Devero was still advancing, leisurely, but she knew his cat-like quickness.

"Stop!" she warned again. "I've told you—"

41

He wasn't stopping. She had known from the start that he would not. Now she gripped the chair tighter, swung it up suddenly, high above her head. Then she brought it crashing down with all her strength, full upon him. She was hardly aware that the wild scream ringing in her ears was issuing from her own throat.

The chair shattered to wreckage, smashing over and around his head, down to his shoulders, to his waist. Still he came on. There was blood on his face now, streaming from an ugly cut over one eye, dripping down across his mouth. She could taste that blood, salty on her lips, as he held her in his arms and his own mouth was upon hers, hungry, savage. Then something seemed to burst in her head, a torment which had been building there for days, and darkness swept over her; she went limp in his arms.

- 9 -

THEY WERE hurrying, hurrying. Never pausing longer than was necessary to graze tired cayuses, to snatch a little sleep for themselves, and not much of that. Urgency drove North like a spur. It was his conviction that horseflesh was cheap, and when worn out could be replaced. As for men, any who rode with him must be able to keep up. They could doze in the saddle, or not at all.

Noland Doll matched him mile for mile as they drove steadily south. To Texas, and on without a pause. What thoughts might fester behind the rocky face of Rawe North Doll could only guess at. But the harsh overtones of them showed constantly.

They were deep in Texas before he showed signs of taking a breather. The Leon ran here, narrow and turbulent. Weeks were behind them since they had turned down from Kansas, and in the north winter would be fastening its relentless grip upon the land. Here the air was humid, crowding in lungs, crawling in lines of sweat down a man's face, itching his back. There was no wind now, as there had been before. Noland Doll had hated the wind, but now he felt its lack. As though they had left a friend behind, were alien in a strange land.

42

Which was odd, for he was Texas raised. But time and distance could change a man. This was his first trip back since before the war. Texas, too, was changed. He had heard plenty of reports of poverty where plenty had reigned, of misery in a land once flowing with milk and honey. But reports were intangibles. Reality could be a noose about your neck.

Natives, who had never drifted as he had done, spoke hopefully where, half a year before, there had been only despair and hopelessness. Now there was a promise like a rainbow in the skies to the north of them.

Cattle were everywhere, here in Texas—mavericks from the years when markets had vanished, and owners or crews had marched to drums or died to note of fife. The brush was full of cattle.

A year before they had been all but worthless. Now they sold for three dollars a head, having tripled in price in half a year. There was promise that they would triple again, and hope burned anew in the hearts of men.

But it was mostly the promise of hope, not yet become reality. There had been a town on this ground, a decade before. Now there was one building, where a man could buy liquor or food, if he had the price. Or get a bed of sorts, and play a game of cards. Rawe North made an abrupt decision.

"There's money here, Noll," he said. "I think we could use some of it."

Doll shrugged. He didn't like the feel of this expedition, which was strange, since it was pretty much the sort of thing to which he had grown accustomed. Knowing North, he had been aware from the start that this would be a desperate venture. Maybe it was the fact that wilderness had reclaimed a land once half civilized that depressed him. He had grown accustomed to seeing that trend reversed. But he said nothing.

With the coming of night, the lone building took on a new aspect. Doll had expected half a score of men, at most, to congregate here. But riders were drifting in like shadows, until at least thirty were clustered about as the game got under way, Rawe North's face was intent and smiling. It was a rare thing to see North smile. About the only time he ever did was when he played poker.

Maybe that was because he almost always won. There was incredible dexterity in the way his long fingers manipulated the cards, a smoothness to rival the professional gambler. Beyond that, those who knew Rawe North seldom ventured an opinion. They contented themselves with the remark that he had a lot of luck with the cards. If they were losers, they usually took their losses with a good grace and pulled out of the game.

Tonight was no exception, so far as the luck was concerned. North was winning. As the game progressed the stakes grew high. Poverty might be the lot for Texas, but there was money in this room. Money out of Texas, but not for Texans. It was a difference well known and not too subtle. Tonight it seemed mostly to belong to a man named Garwood. For the first half-hour Doll watched him, puzzled. He was accepted by these others, but there was something different about him. Then he caught a whisper, and understood. Carpetbagger.

That accounted for his having money, for his sureness. But it didn't account for his acceptance by these others. And then Doll began to understand that, too, and to feel the tension building up in the room.

Go where you would, there were always men for sale. You could buy them as you bought a herd of cattle, and about as cheap, that kind. Garwood had taken the precaution to purchase protection for himself in the country which he exploited.

He wasn't taking it too well as the evening wore on and North continued to win. But Garwood played a careful game, not alone of cards. He had a flat, blank face, devoid of expression as a wiped plate. Now he leaned back in his chair and spoke.

"Luck seems to be with you tonight, Mr. North. A lot of luck."

North smiled again. He could afford to, considering what he had won already.

"I can't complain," he acknowledged.

"I can," Garwood sighed. "I wouldn't go so far as to accuse you of cheating, Mr. North—not that. Though I've known men from up north to have few scruples, here among us Texans."

Doll could feel the chill, as though a door had opened. None had, and the smoke-filled room was still humid, so that as a precaution he wiped the sweat from his eyes and carefully rubbed the palm of his gunhand. As he had guessed, Garwood was clever. He had a part of this crowd on his side, and he was subtly identifying himself with them, painting North as the interloper. He wanted to be sure of where he stood, of what was behind him.

Doll sucked in his breath. Garwood might be clever, but so was North. The carpetbagger had underestimated him, judging solely by appearance, by the fact that they were down from Kansas. The smile had been wiped off North's face.

"Speakin' of Texans," he said, "there's men in this room know I was spawned on the Brazos. . . . Like you say, no real Texan likes a carpetbagger."

Doll waited, while the silence crowded and the smoke shimmered. Then he expelled his breath again. There would be no fight—not now. Color was a thin painting under the flat face of the carpetbagger, but he had learned to bide his time, to take no risks which could be avoided. There were more men in this room against him than for him, though the odds were close.

"Seems like we're in agreement," he commented. "Only I've had enough, and it's quite a ride home."

North gathered up his winnings. Several thousand dollars. They had arranged for a room, and they went to it, but Doll had no need to suggest what was in his mind.

"We'll slip out the window, get our cayuses and keep on ridin'," North whispered. "He'll be back—soon as he gathers more of his kind and figures the others have gone home. But he won't find us here."

Only once did he refer to the game, as, miles down the trail, they prepared to roll in their blankets for a few brief hours of sleep.

"I told you I'd get money down this way, Doll. Working capital. All a man needs do is collect."

45

LATE the next afternoon they came upon a sure sign of what they sought—a long filigree of dust rising and hanging. A trail herd on the move. Two thousand head, Doll estimated swiftly, when at length they came up to them. with nine men driving them, one chuck wagon following. A fair-sized bunch to trail north, though this was late in the year for a drive.

. But they were planning a winter drive when they had gathered a herd. That might be a move of desperation, but Rawe North liked any kind of a gamble if it promised a profit.

North was studying. not the cattle, but the men. He had lost a crew, a range and several herds because of a new trick used against him. If it had worked for other men it could work for him. In fact, the more he considered it, the better he had liked the possibilities. He swung his horse now to where two riders rode a little apart from the others, and his face lightened. Here was luck. He lifted a hand, greeting them familiarly.

"Hi, Ames," he called. "And you, Rowe. Been a long time since I've seen such an ugly pair of horsethieves!"

Their faces lit up in turn at sight of North and his affectionately insulting hail. These were men he'd ridden with before.

Ames was a chunky man with a shaggy head of grizzly hair. There was thick hair on his hands and arms. Rowe, by contrast, was tall, beardless, bald as an egg. But both men had a look about them which, once seen, was unmistakable. The look of men not much at ease in any one place for long at a time. There was always a reason for that—somewhere behind.

"What you doing down this way?" Ames asked, once the greeting had been returned. "Thought you had acquired yourself a spread in Kansas, Rawe?"

"I have," North agreed. "Where you going with this herd, feller?"

Ames jerked his head to indicate the trail they'd come.

"Headin' north," he said. "Poor time of year for it, but

that ain't our funeral. These belong to a man named Pleasant. We've been ten days gettin' this far. He'll be along in another week or so. Busted. Got these scraped together. Aims to make him a new start somewhere up above."

It was a familiar story. North's eyes were speculative.

"Not a bad bunch of cattle," he commented. "And you boys are on the move too, eh?"

"A man has to eat," Ames said flatly. "The farther south you go, the worse things are. He promised us pay—later."

A crooked smile twisted across Rowe's face.

"Yeah. And Ames wanted to get out of Texas. Figgered some other climate might be healthier."

The hairy man nodded without rancor.

"That was one reason," he conceded.

North had turned to look toward the other riders.

"Friends of yours?"

"Some of them."

"How'd you like double pay all the way to Kansas—and a steady job when you get there?"

They exchanged glances, hesitated, then nodded.

"You got somethin' in mind, North?"

"I could use that bunch of beef," North retorted. "How many of the others will go along with you?"

A startled light glowed for an instant in Rowe's eyes, faded.

"Ain't that a mite high-handed?"

"I'm offerin' you double pay," North reminded. "How about it?"

"We-el," Ames scratched his ear speculatively, "I been doubtful of where we'd get, drivin' into the teeth of winter. But with you in charge—I reckon we could go to hell or the plumb opposite an' fight a way through. I'm willin'."

"Two of the others ain't likely to agree," Rowe calculated. "I think mebby the others will."

"We'll talk to them," North said. "Your pay starts as of ten days ago. And here's your first month's wages."

He pulled a roll of bills from his pocket, money which Garwood had unwillingly furnished the night before. Their eyes lighted greedily at sight of real cash. Both accepted their share avidly, noting that the roll was scarcely diminished. With it held openly in his hand, North rode to where

47

the others were gathering, leaving the herd momentarily to drift.

"You talk to 'em, Ames," he suggested.

Ames wasted no words.

"This is Rawe North from Kansas," he said. "Born a Texan, and now he's got the biggest spread north of here. These cattle stand just one chance of gettin through at all, a winter drive—if he rods the herd. Which he's going to do. Double pay for every man that works for him, startin' ten days back—and the first month's wages now, cash! I'm stringin' along, me and Rowe. You boys wasn't born yesterday, I take it?"

There was a minute of startled silence. Accustomed as most of them were to high-handed methods, this cool appropriation of another man's herd in his absence, the buying of his crew, was pretty strong medicine. But it had been worked against him, and already North, sure of himself, was counting out the money.

"Come and get it," he invited.

It was not to be so easy. None of them stirred, and one spoke up angrily.

"Let's get this straight! Are you buyin' this herd from Pleasant—or stealin' them?"

North's eyes were frosty.

"I don't like that word!"

"And I don't like Yankee thieves," the other man retorted hotly. "There's been too damn much of this sort of thing already."

"Like I told you, North ain't no Yankee," Ames said placatingly. "He's a Texan himself."

"Texan, is he? With a spread in Yankee country? Sounds like he's caught the habit, comin' down here to steal from honest men—"

"I've listened to enough of that talk," North warned. "Either you men take my pay and work for me—or you don't. Make your choice!"

The rebellious one reined his horse angrily back. After a moment, one other man rode to join him. But the rest of the crew, after a brief hesitation, did what Ames had predicted. They came over to take their money and join with them. North had a way of picking men.

48

"You're a fine bunch!" the rebel raged. "Dirty traitors! Wait'll we tell Pleasant what's happened to his herd. You won't be able to get away with this. They'll catch and hang you 'fore you get out of Texas—"

"Do you think we'd be such fools?" North demanded. "You had a chance to make your choice. But you'll carry no word away from here."

Panic leaped to the eyes of the man who had come to side the rebellious puncher. Both of them went for their guns. But Noland Doll had come prepared for this, and his gun matched North's for speed. The puncher who had voiced protest had his iron clear of leather, but that was all. His companion did not get that far.

It was an impressive demonstration, if any of their new-hired crew should be in need of bolstering. North coolly punched out the empty shell, replaced it with a fresh cartridge, and holstered his gun.

"Bury them here," he instructed. "Then drive the herd across it."

That was ancient practice, to hide a grave from the Indians. Here there was no threat of that nature, but the reason was as obvious. The job was done, and in silence. North busied himself with ascertaining that the chuck wagon was well stocked.

"You'll be in charge here and rod this herd, Ames," he instructed. "Drift along easy for a while. There'll be more dogies before long, to build the herd up. And Noll and I will soon join you."

"What about a road iron?" Ames asked.

"We'll change no brands till we get to Kansas. Keep your eyes open—and your guns handy. But I hardly need to tell you that. Come on, Noll. This is just a starter."

- 11 -

Doll was glad of the rain. It had come up swiftly, almost a deluge, soaking them instantly. But he felt the need of a washing. He had guessed pretty well what would lie ahead of them on this journey, but the actuality was always worse. He had felt sick, as they filled that double grave, and he knew

49

he'd have no appetite for supper. The rain seemed to help, as though drawing a curtain between them and what had been.

Not that any of it was new. He had trailed his cayuse after Rawe North's star because North did things in a big way. You didn't corral fifteen thousand head of cattle, and the range to run them on, in a night. Not by conventional methods.

It had taken five years to build up the Rail Road brand from scratch. But this time North was in a hurry. He had no added five years to waste, and his methods were those which he and others had tried and found workable, but on a bigger, grimmer scale.

This crew that he had appropriated could be depended on. They wouldn't sell out again. Any man could do that, once. After that, his very life depended on sticking with the man who had purchased him. When North returned to Kansas, he aimed to have a salty crew who would follow him to hell, if necessary. Some of them probably didn't realize what they were letting themselves in for. Learning, it would be too late to change.

Down trail again, and here was more luck, ready-made for such a man as North. Here was a bawling mass of longhorns, held loosely across half a dozen miles. No need to ask what was toward, for a Texan. The wild herds had multiplied during the war years. The brush was thick with them, though many had been gathered in this last year or so. But plenty more waited for whoever could haze them out from among the slashing thorns and put his iron on them.

Four thousand head had been rounded up by forty men, and held. A few more were still being gathered, but these would be ready to roll gradually north on the heels of winter; north to land beyond the line of steel now bisecting Kansas.

As was to be expected, the owner was a carpetbagger. Himself far away and safe in the capital, bending sullen but helpless men to do his will.

North eyed the herd, and Doll caught the gleam in his eyes.

"There's a town on below here," North commented. "Longhorn. We'll get ourselves a crew—and then we'll come back!"

No need to ask what he meant. Hijacking the herd

wouldn't be too hard. Men would work for a carpetbagger, but their loyalty was thin. Yet the implications caused Doll to shake his head. A man who lived at the capital and directed from there would have a long arm and a vengeful one. And here they were deep down in Texas. Taking the herd would be easy, as compared with getting out with it.

Longhorn was old, but most of it was new. There had been few in the town a year before. The boom in cattle had brought it up overnight like a mushroom. Or perhaps a toadstool. Doll decided, considering it. Amid all its squalor, one saloon was outstanding, bigger, more garish. It bore, for this inland country, a strange name: The Paddle Wheel.

They stabled their horses, and North paused, putting a match to a long cigar. His eyes fixed on the sign above the door.

"The Paddle Wheel," he repeated. "There was a Paddle Wheel in St. Louis. . . . Let's go in."

His craggy face was wiped clean of expression, but the name had jarred him. For the most part, he had taught himself not to think of Kansas, nor allow his thoughts to dwell on Marian Breen. He had realized, belatedly, that he had acted badly in leaving her the way he had. She would, of course, turn back as soon as she saw the burned ground and gauged the extent of catastrophe. She had come to Kansas with the clear understanding that he was the biggest man and the richest in all that part of the country. She had made it plain, back in St. Louis, that she was marrying him only because of his possessions.

It was simple, but not, he knew now, that simple. He had owed her something for coming, and it would not be easy to explain his actions when he saw her again. Nostalgia was like a sharp blade turned in a half healed wound now. That tawny, old-gold hair which crowned her high-held head, the deep sweetness of her voice when she sang—

Always it had been a business proposition between them, but he knew, with bitter sharpness, that it was more than that with him. There had been other women possessed of beauty and grace, who could preside over a palace such as he had built. Women whom he had given scarcely a second glance. . . .

51

Now, if she had married Tripp Devero, because he was in turn the big man along the Arkansas—

Next time we meet, Devero, I'll have to kill you, he thought. *Whatever has happened, whatever does—nothing will change that!*

He felt wild hatred surge in him, a feeling which he had carefully kept bottled up. Such strong emotion could disturb a man's thinking, spoil his coolness of calculation, lead him to ruin. He'd seen it happen to others and guarded against it, keeping a tight rein on himself. But it was there—so savage that it half sickened him with the intensity of its bitterness. This was what the name of a far-off saloon could do to him. . . .

He had himself under control as they walked in and up to the bar. And then he received a second shock.

There were women here—not that there was anything unusual about that. But one of them was familiar. He stared at her, and saw that she was looking back at him with that same amazement, and that drove away the last bit of doubt. This girl had been in the Paddle Wheel at St. Louis. He'd never paid much attention to her, but that hair, like smoke-filled flame, was distinctive. What was her name—Alice—no, Altie—that was it. Altie.

"How did you get here?" he demanded abruptly, crossing to her.

There was a roughness in this man to match his exterior. Altie had sensed it back in St. Louis. Now she felt it like a slap in the face. She looked about appealingly, and her eyes met those of Doll for a moment. They seemed to steady her as she answered.

"Why, I—I just drifted here," she explained. "The old place was all broken up—after that night."

"You're Altie, aren't you?" North's voice was less gruff. "Seeing you here surprised me."

"It surprised me too, to—to see you here," Altie faltered. "I thought you'd be in Kansas with Marian."

From the look on his face she knew that she had said the wrong thing. North turned abruptly and walked to the bar, but Doll lingered. Something about the hurt look in this girl's eyes, the way she had spoken Marian's name, caught his attention.

52

"Let's sit down," he suggested. "I'll buy a drink. I—I'd like to talk to you."

She agreed, abstractedly. Studying him for a moment, then looking to where North stood.

"You're with him?" she asked.

"I'm his foreman."

"And his friend?"

Doll considered that, and nodded.

"I suppose so," he agreed. "You—you knew him before?"

"I worked in the Paddle Wheel in St. Louis, while Marian was there," Altie said. "I guess that was what made me suggest the name for this place."

"What happened there?" Doll asked. "I never heard."

"Mr. North said that he was going to take Marian away. Pete Hartse said no. He was the boss. They fought. Then Mr. Devero shot Pete to prevent him knifing Mr. North."

This was news to Doll. He pondered it, still not understanding. Now she was questioning in turn, her voice eager.

"Where's Marian?" she asked. "What happened to her? I—I hope nothing's wrong."

"There's plenty wrong," Doll retorted. "Devero struck—wiped out the ranch, burned the range." For some reason which he did not quite understand, he went on to explain in some detail what he knew—how he had ridden to tell North, his single glimpse of the Thrush, and of how North had ridden away with him, not going back.

"I've never said much to him about it," he confessed. "But it's a play I can't figure. If she came clear out there to marry him—then for him to go off and leave her that way—" He shook his head.

"He thought she wouldn't marry him, with everything gone," Altie explained.

"Well, at least I'd have found out," Doll exploded. "Wouldn't she?" he added.

Altie shook her head, tracing patterns on the table top with one finger, where liquor had been spilled.

"I don't know," she confessed. "Marian is my best friend, about the only real friend I had. I—I never did understand her, but I liked her. I don't think he understood her, either." She looked up at him with a quick smile. "You know my name, but you haven't told me yours."

He hesitated, then blurted it out.

"You'll laugh, of course. It's Doll—Noland Doll."

"Why should I laugh?" she demanded. "I—I rather like it."

"You do?" He found himself unaccountably eager. "Mostly, I have to lick a man—when I tell it. And women—"

"People are mostly mean, I guess, aren't they?" Altie nodded, and he saw the disillusion in her eyes. "At least, that's the way I've found them."

To his surprise, Doll found that he enjoyed talking to this girl. Usually he was ill at ease with women, unsure of himself. Altie was friendly, like a man, sympathetic. Maybe it was because she was the friend of Marian Breen. Not that he knew Marian, but it was a link of sorts, and it seemed to make a difference. He felt a twinge of regret when finally he saw that North was ready to go.

"I—I hope I'll see you again," he blurted. "I like to talk to you."

"I like you too, Doll," Altie agreed. "I'll be here, of course."

He was relieved that North did not mention her. He seemed to have lost all interest in her after that first question or so. He had not wasted his evening. Out of the crowd half a score of men now took his pay.

"They'll get me more of a crew in the next couple of days," he added. "We'll wait till there's fifty. A little rest will do us no harm."

Doll had no need to ask him what he meant. He knew. That big herd of mavericks was to be their booty. They, with the two thousand that had belonged to Pleasant, would make six thousand head. A huge bunch to trail north, the sizable foundation of a new fortune.

Probably it could be done, even with winter blowing across the vast sweep of land in between. If anyone could do it, Rawe North was the man. This was still a lawless country, and plenty of men got away with murder. A change was coming, which would presently make such high-handed methods impossible. Right now, however, law was little more than a shadow.

Oddly, Doll found a growing distaste in himself. Once he hadn't boggled at such methods. Plenty of old-timers, re-

54

spected men in their community now, had founded their fortunes in just such a manner. But somehow he was coming to hate it.

The trouble was that he was in too far to turn now. And there was one good thing. They would be here for a couple of days. He'd get to see Altie again.

That, too, was strange. That he should wish to see her. But in her he sensed a spirit akin to his own. Loneliness, and circumstances which had crowded her gradually into a way not of her choosing nor liking. He was like that now, caught —as were the men with that herd which had belonged to Pleasant, hired by North and now inexorably in his power. They had really had no choice, any more than the pair who had refused. It had been that or die. Those two had kept their honor clean. But of what use was that when you were dead?

He'd never thought much about anything like that before, and it was confusing. Maybe they'd been smart, at that. Now their troubles were over. What on earth had set him to thinking such thoughts? Just meeting with a girl—

He had a room tonight, and a bed instead of a blanket. A ceiling overhead instead of stars. And he couldn't sleep for the softness of it, nor for thinking. Wild thoughts which were alien but not unwelcome. Notions which startled him. You couldn't take a woman along—not on such a trail. Still—

- 12 -

NORTH had been out of town for part of the day. His temper, when he came into the Paddle Wheel, was like his name. He scowled at Doll where he talked with Altie.

"Don't go gettin' mixed up in anything," he warned. "We've got to watch our step down here, if we want to get out of this country with whole skins."

Doll's own temper had shortened during the day. Despite lying long awake the night before, he had found no satisfactory solution for the problem which plagued him, and the day had only made it worse.

"What's chewin' on you now?" he demanded. "You cookin' some new deal?"

"That's the devil of it," North confessed. "This one's

clean as a cat's whiskers. You've heard of Jim McLane?"

"Everybody's heard of him that ever heard of Texas," Doll retorted, without much exaggeration. Jim McLane was an old-timer in the region—a man with fiery temper and unpredictable moods. But he was so unfalteringly honest, so scrupulous in both his business and private life, that men spoke of him with pride, almost with affection. Jim McLane was not merely of Texas. He *was* Texas—in both its turbulence and its honor.

"You ain't tryin' to put nothin' over on *him*, are you?" Doll demanded. "You do that an' we never will get out alive."

"I told you this was a straight deal," North growled. "He's got a thousand head of cattle for sale, and I want to buy them. Offered him the cash. But he's holdin' back on account of me being from Kansas. And I need that herd."

Doll viewed him curiously. That North had some scheme in mind he had not the slightest doubt. There were tens of thousands of cattle for sale for cash, and little to choose between any of them for quality.

"I'm going to try again," North added. "I've got to find a way to soften him up. But remember what I told you."

Doll ate his supper alone in a restaurant, too despondent even to wonder particularly what North was up to. Then, though he knew that it was a foolish thing to do, he wandered back to the Paddle Wheel. For a while he sat at a table by himself, morose and wondering what was wrong with him. Altie was not in the room.

Something roused him, and he knew that he had dozed. Night lay outside the windows, the lamps had been lighted inside. And Altie had appeared.

It was that which had awakened him, he knew now. She was struggling in the grasp of a bearded giant of a man, who was laughing and trying to kiss her.

That was nothing new in such a place as this. Nor was it any of his business. Doll knew that, but he was on his feet and running, so quickly as to draw the startled gaze of the other inmates of the saloon. He paid no attention to them. His hand fell on the bearded man's arm, wrenching him back.

"Let her alone," he said thickly.

The big man—he was very young for all his heavy beard

56

—released her, and Altie staggered back, her eyes filled with dismay.

"It's all right," she gasped.

"The hell it is," the bearded man rasped. He had paused for a moment to survey this stranger who dared to interfere with him, amazement in his face. Now, without warning, he lunged at Doll, big hands outreaching. Altie screamed.

To the onlookers it looked much as it did to her—as though this rash stranger would have no chance at all. But Basque and Creole made a hot and dangerous combination. Noland Doll laughed. Here at last was something that he could do—a vent for the ferment which had been storing up in him for the last few days. He danced lightly aside, and the flat of his hand popped like a pistol-shot across the big man's face.

It was like a bull trying to gore a hound which snapped at its heels. The big man was quick, but he was no match for the lithe speed of Doll. Doll hit him almost at will and where he pleased. He would dart in, and the solid thud of his blows told how hard they were. At first they had little effect, save to increase the savagery building up in the other man. His rushes became wilder, even less effective. Doll was playing with him, but it was ruthless play, like that of a cat with the victim it intended to feast upon.

Now one of the big man's eyes was closing, then the other. Blood smeared his face, which was purpling, puffing grotesquely. His rushes had given way to a dazed sort of pivoting on his feet, while he stood like a befuddled grizzly and tried to ward off the rushes of an antagonist that he now could scarcely see. And yet he remained on his feet, refusing to go down despite the punishment he had taken.

The door surged open and three men burst in. One of them wore the badge of a town marshal.

"What's going on here?" he demanded, and advanced upon Doll. "You can't do that in this town—"

"Who's going to stop me?" Doll demanded, and looked at the startled marshal over the leveled barrel of his revolver.

No man had seen that draw. They had been watching, but such a speed was rare, even in this land where fast guns were the rule. Like the nudge of a trout, taking bait from a hook before the fisherman knew it was striking.

And then the door had opened again, and two more men came into the saloon. Doll suddenly felt cold. One of them was Rawe North. The man with him, wearing a plaid shirt and bristling fiery whiskers, could be none other than Jim McLane. Those twin trademarks were known all over Texas.

The marshal was still staring at the gun, at the unwinking black eyes behind it. He tried to bluster.

"We hang men for less than that in this town," he threatened. "Put up that gun!"

"And I've killed men for less," Doll retorted flatly, and saw North advancing, scowling. His voice rapped across the silence.

"What's going on here, anyway? Noland, put up that gun! What the devil are you up to?"

Doll held the gun steady. The marshal explained volubly.

"He comes in here and picks a fight with Colin Welch. Then he drags a gun on me—"

Thunderous laughter shook the room. Mirth which bellowed up from a mighty chest and rolled in an engulfing tide to fill the room and seep out to the street beyond. Gargantuan laughter from the throat of Jim McLane. His outflaring whiskers bristled like the horns of a lead steer.

"Light of Mars, that I should live to see this day!" he chuckled. "A year now I've watched Colin Welch bully this town and lord it over better men, as though he was something the Lord had made special, instead of a mistake of creation! And tonight comes a man half his size who whittles him down to size, whereat the law must come yapping like a mongrel cur to save him! Light of Mars, but 'tis a good world yet!"

He swung suddenly on the marshal, and a scowl replaced the mirth in his face.

"Take him out of here and put him to bed," he roared. "And let me hear no word of arrestin' a man who beats him in fair fight! Any man should be grateful—and most of them will be, I've no doubt. Man, 'tis Jim McLane would be proud to shake your hand!"

His own big paw was seizing Doll's and pumping it as Doll holstered the gun, and the marshal, abashed as a schoolboy, was leading Welch away without a backward glance, while the scowl was gone from North's face.

Nothing then would do but that there must be a round of drinks, and the crowd, carefully neutral up to this point, all hastened to congratulate him. Which was well enough, except that he had scarcely a chance then for a word with Altie, though her eyes were luminous when she did thank him.

"You shouldn't have interfered," she said. "Not on my account."

"I'll have no man bothering you," Doll declared. "Maybe now they'll know better."

"Maybe," Altie agreed. "Though I didn't care—before." She looked at him, confused by what her tongue had confessed, and turned and hurried away. North was in high good humor as they returned to their room.

"That was a good piece of work you did, Noll," he commended. "And did it tickle Old Whiskers! I'd worked on him all evening again, and still he wouldn't give me a straight answer. But the last thing he said was to come out and see him in the morning. And you'll go along. He'll sell now."

That proved to be true prophecy. They rode to McLane's Lone Star ranch, half a dozen miles from the town, where the thousand head were gathered. He greeted them warmly, chuckling in retrospect over what had happened the evening before.

"That Colin Welch has been askin' to be curried a right long time," he said. "Light of Mars! He comes in here and acts like a king, because his carpetbagger father holds Texas in his hands like a sack of grapes and twists and squeezes the juice out, also the life of those who dare resist him! Defeated we may be, but men we are still—or a few are, praise God! I was fearful you were another yellow-belly in with the carpetbagger crowd, North, just because you live among the Yankees. Now I know better. We can do business."

He nodded shaggy beard toward the herd, bellowed for a moment with laughter and was as swiftly sober again.

"There's the thousand head you said you wanted, and at the price you agreed to pay—three thousand dollars. A steal it is, considering what you'll get for them when you reach the railroad, but to you it's fair."

"And here's the money," North agreed, and handed it over in a wad. "Count it to be sure it's right. Also here's a bill of sale I wrote out this morning, if you'll sign it."

McLane accepted the money, laughing again until the tears trickled into his whiskers.

"Sure of yourself, weren't you?" he chuckled. "But after last night, well you knew you held me in the hollow of your hand!" While he thumbed the bills, Doll read the bill of sale, which he was to sign as a witness.

It was clear and simple enough. For $3,000 cash paid, Jim McLane sold Rawe North 1,000 head of cattle, composed of various brands or no brand at all. McLane read it and affixed his own signature, and the deal was complete. But Doll was still puzzled as the two of them rode back to town.

"I still don't see why you were so anxious to buy from him," he said. "If you wanted to pay cash, anybody would be glad to sell."

"Sure," North agreed. "But just anybody wouldn't do. Whereas Jim McLane is known all over Texas, and as an honest man. We'll start up trail with them in the morning."

That was what Doll had figured. What he was suddenly afraid of. Not that he had any desire to linger here, so far as the country itself was concerned. He had had no intimation that the big man was Colin Welch, and through his father's influence a power in Texas, before tangling with him. Even had he known, it would have made no difference.

But Welch would be vengeful, there was little doubt of that. After he'd gone, too, Welch would be certain to thrust his attentions on Altie, if for no other reason than because she had been the cause of his discomfiture—

"Like blazes he will!" Doll swore, and turned toward the Paddle Wheel.

He had made up his mind. He was crazy, of course—no one needed to tell him that. But sometimes the craziest notions turned out the best. At least, he knew what he wanted.

Altie agreed to go riding with him, when he brought horses. She seemed both surprised and pleased, and for a while they rode almost in silence. It was the first time he had ever ridden with a woman, and he found himself constantly amazed at her. She did not talk much, but the silence was companionable.

"You ride like a cowboy," he said.

"I'd ought to," Altie agreed. "I was just about raised on a horse."

"Then a long trip wouldn't bother you," he blurted.

She looked at him, not understanding.

"What do you mean?"

Doll felt his face go red, but he persisted.

"I mean, why not go back to Kansas with me?" he asked. "We could be married, and—well, I been thinkin' about it a lot. That's what I wanted to talk to you about."

She looked at him strangely, and then he saw her face twist and go soft, and knew that she was crying. He hesitated, uncertain, sure that he had said something wrong, but not knowing what to do about it.

"Aw, now, Altie," he protested. "Don't do that. If I've offended you—I sure didn't mean to—"

"You haven't," she denied, but still did not look at him. "You—I'm crying because I'm happy."

"You—you mean you will?" he demanded eagerly.

Still she did not look at him.

"I'm going to remember this—always," she promised. "It —it's what I've always dreamed about—and hoped for—"

"We can be married right away," Doll insisted. "You won't have to go back there at all—"

This time she did look at him. And shook her head.

"It's awfully nice of you—but of course I can't."

"Can't?" he demanded. "I'd like to know why not."

"You'd ought to know," she said. "It just wouldn't do. I— I like you too much for that."

Doll scowled.

"If you mean—where you work, why, I—I ain't been no plaster saint myself—"

Altie looked away again, but her voice was final.

"I'll always remember this—and you, Noland," she whispered. "I think you're the finest man I've ever known. And it's the nicest thing that's ever happened to me. But—it just wouldn't do. I—I wouldn't be good for you."

- 13 -

FROM that decision Doll had been unable to move her. Altie looked soft and yielding, but on this she was adamant. Finally she turned to him pleadingly.

"Please don't say any more about it, Noland. And don't—don't let's quarrel. This other is so—so wonderful, that I want to remember it just that way. And we—we'll still have this evening—to see each other."

Doll yielded to her urging. He was angry, puzzled, more unsure of himself than he had ever expected to be, but he knew that he didn't want to make things any harder for her. And maybe, at the last minute, she would change her mind.

North wouldn't like it if she did. The idea of taking a woman along on such a drive, one woman among a lot of men, wouldn't appeal to him. He'd figure it as likely to stir up trouble, where already they would have more than they could conveniently handle. But on such a matter as that Doll was minded to handle his own affairs. Once she started with him, he'd look after her, all the way from there on out.

He returned to the Paddle Wheel again as evening settled. North was somewhere in town, busy as usual with the affairs which had brought him here. A part of the new-hired crew had been dispatched to start the thousand head on the move at the crack of dawn. As they passed through the town the rest of them would join up, making a crew of half a hundred. An overwhelming number to be driving such a small herd.

But the herd, as Doll knew, was destined for a fast increase. And they'd need a big, hard-bitten crew to hang onto them, to push them safe out of Texas and along the trail to the Arkansas. North was making sure not only of plenty of men, but that they knew how to use a gun.

Doll's eyes ranged the big room expectantly, and he saw Altie and moved to a table, and she came to join him. Various men nodded in friendly fashion, since his brush with Welch the evening before. But there was a wariness about them as well. They were not forgetting that Welch had the law, such law as there was in Texas, on his side. And back of him a support that was not to be taken lightly. They were accepting Doll, but most of them would draw a breath of relief when he and North rode out of town.

Altie was very quiet. That suited Doll, for he felt the same way. Eyeing her closely, he judged that she had been crying.

"This makes me feel like a skunk," he said miserably. "To come here and make you feel bad, Altie—"

She smiled, so warmly as to take him off guard.

"Make me feel bad?" she echoed. "Where do you get that notion? I haven't felt so—so happy in years."

"Then how about makin' me feel happy, too, by going along with me?" he repeated. "Don't I count for nothin'?"

"I wish you wouldn't put it that way, Noland," she chided. "You just make it hard. You—you know you do count. And that—that's why I can't do it."

It was useless to argue. He saw that, and his liking for her increased. But this didn't need to be final. After they reached Kansas, he could return. And maybe, when she saw how determined he was too, she would change her mind. Thought of that possibility lightened his mood. He grinned at her.

"There's more days coming," he said. "And I don't know that I blame you much. Maybe I was wrong. There's going to be plenty trouble on the drive, all the way to Kansas. And once we get there—there'll be more than ever. But after that's over—"

She looked at him quickly, understanding what he meant, and sudden fresh pain was in her heart, as though a knife twisted there. He meant to return again for her. It was bitter-sweet, and it left her gasping for breath momentarily, and praying—an almost forgotten prayer, long unused, on her lips. But she had to have strength!

It had taken far more courage than he guessed to refuse him already, when her whole being cried out with longing to go. There would be hardship on the trail, but there would be the clean sweep of the wind, fresh air to blow the past away. And him beside her!

Only, of course, nothing could blow the past away, and for that reason she must not go beside him. And if he planned to return—that meant that once more she must be on the move, long before he got back, to make sure that he did not find her when he came. It would take strength to go, severing the last link, the chance of ever seeing him again. But if she waited, she might not have the resolution a second time.

Somehow she forced a smile, and he was looking toward the door, not seeing the quick spasm which had contorted her face. Rawe North was coming in, pausing for a moment to survey the smoke-filled room. Then he had seen them, was picking his way toward their table. She was sorry and glad at the same time to have him come.

North was still in a good mood. Events had marched at his direction today, and he knew that he was in a fair way to attain what he had come after. It took luck, but a man had to know how to ride his luck to get anywhere. When to spur. Well, he was one who knew.

He sat down, pulling out a chair and applying a match to a long cigar. He glanced quizzically at Altie through the smoke.

"You and Doll seem to have hit it off pretty well together," he commented. "I never knew Doll to be a ladies' man before."

"He is a fine man," she said. "And I will always—"

She broke off, her eyes widening. She was looking toward the door, and both men swung instinctively to see. Two men had come through it. One of them was Welch. Though he still carried the marks of the beating which Doll had given him, he was himself again. His eyes were no longer swollen, and he moved with deliberate intent toward their table.

The man beside him was smaller, sandy-haired, and he wore no beard or mustache. But there was that about him which spelled danger. Other patrons of the place veered away from them.

They were paying no attention to anyone else in the room, giving no greetings nor returning any. They stopped at a distance of a few paces, and while Welch's eyes were fixed on Doll, the other man was watching North with the same intentness. It was he who spoke.

"Remember me, North?"

North was suddenly wary.

"You lookin' for trouble, Zip?" he countered.

Zip smiled. At least it would pass for that, but somehow it twisted to a grimace.

"I'm lookin' for you," he amended. "You got out of Texas in the first place because you was scared of me, didn't you? And then you sent men back to kill me—and they figgered they'd done it. So you dared to sneak back then!"

"That's a lie, all of it," North retorted. "When I've any dogs to kill, I do it myself!"

"You called me a liar once before, North. But you never will again. This time I'm going to kill you."

Welch had said nothing. There was no need. Doll knew that he was here for the same purpose. They were sure of

64

themselves, these two. But for his own part he felt no worry. Situations such as this only made him doubly cool and alert. Unlike North, he didn't go out of his way to look for trouble, but when it came, he had never yet been worried by it. North was like him that way. He wasn't afraid.

Zip motioned now to Altie.

"This is between the four of us," he said. "You better get back out of the way."

"Yeah," Welch added. "I don't want you hurt, queenie."

Altie was watching them, her eyes wide and fearful. One hand went to her throat in a halting gesture, and she looked quickly at Doll, then around the room. But no one else would interfere in this. Jim McLane was not in town tonight, and no one else had his courage or wish to take sides.

"Do as he says, Altie," Doll nodded. "It won't take long!"

There was truth in that. She had witnessed such scenes before, and she knew all the signs. There was death in the room, like a monstrous presence waiting to pounce. Death was not always that way. She had seen it come in friendly guise, bringing merciful release. But this which hovered now was deadly cold, relentless as fate.

Her knees felt like wet blotting paper. With a cool nod to the others, Doll stood up and assisted her to her feet, aided her back to the wall. He ignored the others for the moment, turning his back on them. So long as Rawe North watched, he had no fear of treachery.

"You'd better go back to your room, Altie," he suggested. "This won't be pleasant."

She shook her head, standing there at the wall. He turned back, and now it was he who dominated the scene, a mocking asperity in his voice.

"Didn't you have enough last night, Welch? I tried to make it convincing. But if you want more—that's up to you. Only how about all of us stepping outside? There's ladies here—and besides, it messes up the place."

"Ladies, he says!" Welch guffawed. "That's good!"

He exchanged a look with Zip, who nodded slightly.

"We're willin'," Zip agreed. "Outside's as good as any."

It happened then with blinding speed. Before these witnesses, and in the face of that agreement, they had momentarily relaxed their vigilance. North started to rise, to turn, and so was not watching. Doll, in that same instant, was looking toward Altie.

Only she had not relaxed her watch, not even for an instant. Now, with a choking cry, she hurled herself forward, just as guns crashed loud on the pent-up atmosphere of the room. She was in front of him, and by the same token in front of Rawe North as well, between them and the belching guns of the other pair.

Doll spun, and rage was in him like a snake striking. Killing anger, more savage than he had ever known before. Usually, with him, this sort of thing was a game, deadly but dispassionate. Now he saw the red blob on Altie's waist, heard the flesh-crunching impact of the heavy bullet, and then his own gun was in his hand and he was hurling himself forward as he triggered.

North was raging too, as though he had never practiced treachery himself. Shooting, but with a speed not quite to match Doll's in that moment. It was soon over, as Doll had foretold. Altie was crumpling and going down in a heap on the floor, but the other two were hardly an instant behind her. Welch was first, so that Zip sprawled across him, the two of them marking an ungainly X in the middle of the floor.

Choking, Doll dropped to his knees, gently raising Altie's head, his eyes, usually searching, blinded now by unaccustomed tears. After a moment her eyes opened and she looked up at him and the mist of pain cleared as she saw who it was. She even managed to smile.

"Altie!" he choked, and saw how her blood bubbled out at her breast as she breathed. He knew, without telling, that nothing could hold her long now, not even his own arms. Too many times had he seen the effect of a forty-five bullet. And he suspected that she had taken two of them, though he was not certain where the other had hit.

She tried, unsteadily, to raise her hand, to reach his bowed head and caress it, but the effort proved too great and her arm dropped back. Rawe North, coldly efficient, brought a glass half filled with whiskey.

"Drink this," he suggested.

Altie took it gratefully as Doll held it, leaning her head back against his chest. Blood was staining him, but he paid no heed to that. His eyes were savage with hurt as he looked

66

toward the two men sprawled there, dead already, who had done this.

She choked painfully, and he took the glass away. But for a moment it was at North that she looked, not at him.

"I think I—saved you too," she whispered, and both men knew that it was so. "So—I've a right to ask a favor. Be good to Marian, Rawe—make her happy. She was—the only real friend—I ever had."

North made no reply, but his face was sober. Her eyes closed for a moment, and Doll was afraid that she had gone. Then they opened again and, meeting his gaze, her own grew soft.

"This—is best, Noland," she murmured. "Bend close—it's getting dark. Oh—I wanted to go with you! And now—this way—I can. It's better—than I ever hoped for—"

Her voice faltered, and when it came again it was so weak that he had to bend close to hear.

"You've never—kissed me, Noland," she said. "But if you wanted to—once—"

Words were in him, choking him, words which there was no time to speak, which he could not say in any case. But as he kissed her, he had the feeling that she understood what he wanted to tell her. Her smile grew radiant for a moment, and again she sought to lift her hand to touch his face. Then he stood up, lifting her in his arms, there in the sudden and for once completely respectful silence of the room. She had taken the long trail ahead of him.

- 14 -

Few men indeed had ever seen Tripp Devero dismayed, but had there been any to witness now, they would have beheld a badly frightened man. He was still frantically at work, chafing wrists, wetting Marian's forehead and doing other ineffectual things, when Judy and Bud Farris returned to the cook house.

Judy took efficient charge. But there was not much that she could do, as it soon developed. This was no ordinary fainting spell on the part of Marian Breen. She was unconscious, and Judy turned a coldly suspicious eye on Devero.

"What you do to her, anyway?" she demanded.

Devero was deeply contrite.

"I reckon it's all my fault," he admitted. "I tried to kiss her—and she slammed me over the head with that chair. Then, the next thing, she just went limp in my arms, as I caught her. But I sure didn't intend to do anything to upset her this way."

"Who you, anyway," Judy probed, and added shrewdly, "You this Tripp Dev'ro, maybe?"

"Yes, I'm Devero. But I'd sooner cut off my hand—or my head, for that matter—than to do anything to hurt her."

Judy placed a broad palm on Marian's forehead and surveyed him with kindlier eyes.

"Reckon it ain't your fault—much," she said. "She set lot of store by you, from what I make out. She plumb sick—been actin' funny here las' two-three days. Feel how hot she is now."

Devero obeyed, and was startled at the feverish touch. If there was relief in the knowledge that this might not be all his fault, it was wiped away in the conviction that here was grave illness. He made an abrupt decision.

"We've got to get her to a doctor, quick as it can be managed. I'll hitch up the team, and we'll start. You get her ready to travel."

"Guess she as ready as she ever will be," Judy retorted. "Ain't nothin' lef' here but bare wall an' burned ground." She was as much relieved at the prospect of leaving as she was worried at this strange malady which had struck her mistress down.

Devero found Bud Farris outside, holding the horses. He had met Farris once before, and now he was shocked at the change in the man.

"What happened to you?" he demanded, and listened in growing surprise as Farris explained. Bud had made considerable improvement in the last week. The blistered skin was peeling, being replaced by good fresh growth beneath, and most of the festering globules where shot had penetrated were healed. But his eyes were still sore and sightless.

"You'll come along," Devero instructed. "Couldn't leave you here in any case. And it'll do no harm to have a medico look you over."

He harnessed the horses and hitched the team to the wagon, then carried Marian out and made her as comfortable as possible, with Judy to watch over her in the back of the wagon. There was no change that he could see, and his mouth was a tight line as he climbed to the seat again and took up the reins.

A fringe of light green, spring-like in its fairness, overlay the burned country now. Nature was erasing the scar as quickly as possible. As they traveled, there were signs of life again—a bird on the wing, a coyote in the distance. Devero saw both, but had no time for them. He was thankful that he had ridden this way on impulse. But he was bitter with self-reproach for his own conduct, for the part it might have had in bringing this sickness to a head.

He did not stop as night came on, a nearly full moon riding high overhead. There was nothing more mellow than a full autumn moon over the wide expanse of prairie. Tonight he frowned upon it and urged the horses to a steady pace. Judy and Farris slept. The light, shining whitely back through the parted canvas, showed no change in Marian.

He stopped when the edge of the burned strip was reached. The horses ate hungrily, and from his own duffle bag Devero produced cold biscuits, jerky and coffee. The coffee he boiled over a fire of twisted dry grass, and the three of them ate. Devero turned then, swung to the saddle of his own cayuse.

"The team will have to rest before they can go any farther," he said. "I'll be back during the day."

He grudged the delay, but it had one advantage. By cutting north and slightly east from here he'd reach one of the line camps on his own land in the least possible time.

The sun was halfway to its zenith when he reached the camp, and here luck was with him, for there were two men at it. It might as easily have been empty all day or for several days. But a line rider was there, and Big Ben, who acted as foreman in Devero's absence, had just ridden in.

Big Ben, in its way, was a misnomer. Ben was not big. Nor, in all probability, was that his name. He was a little man, almost scrawny, with a past which he considered as being his own business. The teeming heart of London had first looked upon him with as little favor or hope as he in turn had eyed the murky light of the district where he was born.

The years had brought him to Kansas, making of him a cowboy second to none on any range. His nostalgic references to Big Ben in London had given him his name, which suited him well enough. Now he listened gravely to his employer while they shared a breakfast of beefsteak, washed down by more coffee.

"Blimey, if ever I heard the like," Big Ben confessed. His eyes were sharp but kindly. "Reckon you're doing all anybody could," he added. "And it ain't none of it rightly your fault. Be North's, if anybody's, bringin' her to such a place and then leavin' her wi' nary a word. A woman'd worry herself sick sure, that way."

Big Ben had somehow fostered the illusion that he knew a great deal about women. This conclusion, as he had intended, was comforting.

"North's a bigger fool than I thought he was," Devero growled. "To go off and leave her that way." He dismissed the subject for more practical matters. "I'm taking her to a doctor, and looking after her till she's well! No matter how long it takes. You look after things here. I had to let you know."

"Sure," Big Ben agreed. "I'll do that. Anything else?"

"Yes. Find out what the devil happened to North's men—and to his herd. There's something funny there."

"Funny ain't half the word for it," Big Ben grunted. "I been hearin' rumors—" He shook his head, leaving the words hanging in mid-air. They packed fresh provisions and supplies from the stock in the cabin on an extra horse, and Devero turned back.

It was late afternoon when he reached the wagon again. There was no noticeable change in Marian, and his mouth set a little tighter. But the team was in better shape, thanks to the rich pasture they had enjoyed. He hitched them up again and went on, driving for more than half the night, until the moon dipped beyond the horizon, before he stopped.

There were towns closer than Wichita, but none where a doctor lived, so far as he knew. Mostly, in this country, a settler lived or died without benefit of much assistance. Nonetheless, he headed for the nearest town.

As he had feared, there was no medico. But he saw something else which gave him a sudden idea. A tall, shambling

Swede was loitering on the street, chewing a straw and wearing a lost look. Devero crossed to him.

"Hello, Lars," he greeted. "What you doing here?"

Lars Hanson scowled.

"Ay bane tank about the devil," he growled. "And here you come!"

Strangely, Devero grinned at that.

"I reckon I know what you're thinkin' about, Lars," he agreed, "and so I don't blame you for being sore. You were buildin' that big house for North, and then it burned down. And you figure I did it, and put you out of a job."

"That's yoost what ay do figure," Hanson conceded. "Now ay don't have no vork, no money to pay my men, nothing. An' winter comin' on."

"Well, I've got two things to say to you," Devero retorted. "In the first place, whatever folks say, I had nothing to do with burning that house. You can believe me or not, as you like. But since you're out of a job, how about going to my place and putting up a house about like it for me? Big Ben will show you where—just below the little spring off from where my house is now. Hustle it along as fast as you can. Never mind the expense. Ben will see that the lumber and supplies get hauled, and pay your wages as they're due—not at the end of the job. If you can have it done by spring, I'll give you an extra bonus."

Hanson stared, then his face lightened.

"By golly," he exclaimed. "Maybe ay be crazy, maybe you be. But we go to work, yah. Right away."

Devero scribbled an order to his foreman and gave it to him.

"I'll count on you," he said. "Make it good!"

He returned to the wagon and drove on. The next day, heading straight, he reached the railroad.

Here the grade, slight in most places, still showed raw across the land. The twin lines of steel shimmered in the sun, making the prairie seem more lonely by comparison. But a smudge of smoke showed on the western horizon, gradually taking shape as a locomotive and half a dozen cars. The train halted as he flagged it, and they got aboard. The horses he unharnessed and left to look out for themselves. The wagon he left beside the track, its canvas flapping in the wind. The train whistled and got under way again.

There was a change for the better as they approached Wichita. Marian Breen opened her eyes and stirred, though there was no recognition in them. Fever and delirium held her in their grip.

The doctor at Wichita dosed her and listened and shook his head.

"I'll be honest with you," he confessed. "She's plenty sick, but I've never seen anything quite like this in my experience. She still has a lot of fever. We've got to lick that. When it goes down, she ought to be better. But I have a notion that she'll be far from well for quite a while, followin' a sickness such as this. But we'll do the best we can."

He did it, a best good enough to control and gradually abate the fever. With Bud Farris he had better luck. He treated both eyes, and announced that Bud would be able to see out of one of them again.

But as the fever abated, the Thrush showed scant improvement. She was very weak, as the doctor had prophesied, gripped by an apathy which amounted to languor. She knew Devero now, and was grateful, but she seemed to take no interest in life or in living. Worried, Devero consulted the doctor, who confessed to perturbation on his own part.

"Where's she from?" he demanded.

"She came out here from St. Louis."

"Then you better get her back there," the doctor advised. "I don't know just what's been wrong with her—some sort of a fever she picked up somewhere, and it's kind of affected the mind as well as the body. What I mean is, it dragged her down till she's plumb low, and it'll take rest and a long time to build her up. And some sort of a change, one that's pleasant, to kind of jar her out of this mood and make her want to get well again. Like seeing old friends and places she knew.

"Maybe it won't do any good to take her back there," he added honestly. "I don't know. But they've got good doctors there—better'n I am. And it could have a good effect." He grinned faintly.

"It's an old trick with my profession, when we don't know what to do. Recommendin' a change of scenery or climate. If they live, we can take the credit. If a patient dies, we done

72

the best we could. Not that I figure there's any danger of her dyin', you understand. But she ain't getting along the way she should:"

Devero understood. This was a mental illness added to the physical, as the doctor had said. A lost interest in life, due, he figured, to shock and disillusion.

Winter was in full control of the land now. Holding a heyday of white carnival. There was work which should be done, back on his own spread, but he gave no thought to that. They took the train again, this time for St. Louis.

- 15 -

THE THOUSAND longhorns which had belonged to Jim Mc-Lane reached town as the sun was slanting across Texas, having already rolled across half a continent. The herd had started at dawn, according to orders, and having been kept close herded for weeks, they were impatient to push ahead fast. Here at the town the rest of North's big crew joined them. The drive had begun.

Noland Doll rode in silence. Never a talkative man except in rare streaks, he had even less to say now. He had made the preparations, had worked frantically during the night to locate a sky pilot and to see that the funeral was as fine as could be managed. He had gone out in the dark and gathered some late-blooming flowers where he had seen them the previous afternoon, when he and Altie had ridden together.

And in the dawn, as the herd was stirring a few miles away, they had buried her.

He had attended the burial of many men, most of whom had died as suddenly and as violently as she had done. Seldom in this land did death come naturally and in peace. Some of them had been his friends, but never had such a service affected him like this one. Altie had been so wistfully eager, she had ridden so well only the day before. His face was grim with the twisting pain inside him.

By the time they reached where the big herd was being gathered, the thousand had run off their wildness, were moving sedately as crows at a convention. The afternoon was hot, sultry as midsummer. Flies buzzed and clung in a sticky torment. Clouds piled across the west, the breeze that had stirred at noon was held in abeyance as if to gather its strength.

North rode ahead, Doll beside him. The feel of storm was in the air, and there would be trouble as sure as the sun went down. Doll was in a mood to welcome it. If he should stop a bullet himself, it would be a friendly thing. He didn't know much about such matters, but maybe it was as the sky pilot had said. That there was another chance for those who had not done too well here, that life did not end with death. If it really opened a door to a new life beyond, maybe he could find Altie beyond that door. Altie, who had gone from him so quickly, and who had had so little here.

Now the greater herd was ahead, slow dust above them like a haze. North gave instructions for the smaller bunch to be halted, ten men to watch it. Forty others rode ahead with Doll and himself, men who knew what their job would be and were willing to do it. They stopped in turn at the brush by the creek, to wait there out of sight until North signaled them to come ahead. He and Doll rode out beyond the creek.

Here was the herd, in process of gathering for weeks at the orders of a Yankee. Three men jogged to meet them, grinning.

"We've been workin' among the crew, like you told us to," one, whom North greeted as Medlow, reported. "There's forty here, all told. Twenty we can vouch for. They've already got your pay in their pockets, and know their job. Likewise they've signed on for the drive to Kansas, like you ordered.

"Of the others—well, sev'ral will be sure to be against us. Some of them natural, some because they're workin' for the Yankee to start with. Part of the twenty will side with us when it's put up to them. But where they're doubtful, we ain't said nothing, like you ordered."

"Good," North agreed. "Let's talk to that bunch."

"The men we can depend on are holdin' the herd," Medlow went on. "I fixed that. The others are gathered over there. I told 'em there was somethin' important comin' up."

"That's fine," North said again, and they rode to where the score of men waited. He lifted an arm to tip back his hat,

74

and Doll knew that was a signal to the two score beyond the brush. Medlow introduced them.

"This here is Rawe North, a Texas man with a ranch in Kansas," he said, "and his foreman, Noland Doll. North has somethin' to say to you."

"I'll make it brief," North promised. "Most of you men have been doing a job that you don't like. What I mean is, roundin' up this herd for a Yankee carpetbagger. You've done it for wages, because a man has to eat. And we all know who controls the money in Texas, these days. But from now on, you'll be workin' for me, not for him."

One man bristled promptly. He had been lounging on the ground, leaning on an elbow, chewing a spear of grass. Now he bounced to his feet.

"You bought the herd?" he demanded. "And whether you have or not, who give you license to run off at the mouth that way? We been doing the job for pay, sure, but when we take a man's wages, we don't stand for somebody else slurrin' him!"

Some of the others drew closer to him, approvingly. North lifted a sardonic shoulder.

"Ain't that touchin', now!" he sneered. "I knew he had some of his own kind here, masqueradin' as Texans. But whether you like what I said or not, this is my herd now. Those of you who'd like to work for me, and go on to Kansas, have got a job. We're startin' now. And it'll pay you to work for me."

"You mean you've bought this herd?" the rebel asked doubtfully.

"How else would I get them?" North retorted. "Now, how many of you want to sign up for the drive?"

The other man was unconvinced.

"You got a bill of sale to show you own 'em?" he demanded.

"Right here," North agreed cheerfully. "Want a look at it?"

"I sure do." The rebel pushed forward, shoving back his hat, and Doll's heart sank. North was making a good bluff, but apparently this man could read. The odds had been against that. Doll could respect loyalty in a man.

75

North held out the bill of sale, lounging in the saddle. The other man peered at it, and his face reddened angrily.

"It's just as I thought," he exclaimed, turning to the others. "This ain't for this bunch at all. He's tryin' to steal the herd. And I, for one, ain't going to stand for it!"

"What you aimin' to do?" North's voice was amused. He'd hoped to avoid trouble, but had been ready for it.

"Fight," was the prompt report. "We'll stop you. Call the rest of the boys," he added. "Those with the herd—"

"Those with the herd," North informed him, "have already signed up and are takin' my pay. That's why they're guardin' the bunch now. And take a look behind you."

The handful of rebels turned, and some of the pugnacity went out of them at sight of the men emerging from the brush by the creek. They looked like a small army.

"I've got a big herd to move to the Arkansas," North went on. "Seven thousand head in all. So I've got a big crew to move them—and to fight when we have to. But you fellows can make up your minds. I don't want anybody along—or taking my pay—who don't have their heart in it. I've got plenty of men without that sort."

The leader of the little group hesitated, then squared his shoulders again.

"That's the way I feel too," he grunted. "I won't work for a man I don't like—nor a thief. You can count me out!"

Some hesitated uneasily. The clouds had been building up fast in the last few minutes, and now they blotted away the late afternoon sun. A rumble of thunder growled.

Another man crossed to stand with the rebel. Inspired by that gesture, others followed, until there were six of them. The remainder of the twenty, after some hesitation, moved to the other side, along with North and Doll.

"Once a crew of honest men catch up with you, we'll know how to deal with cattle thieves," the rebel said bitingly. "But traitors will get somethin' special!"

"And fools will get it now!" North said roughly. "All right, boys, they're askin' for it!"

He lifted his hand again, and this was the signal. Doll took no part. He had suddenly lost all stomach for that sort of thing. This was butchery—or North intended it for that.

The rebellious six, taken by surprise, were not caught en-

76

tirely off guard. They scattered, shooting as they ran, and a couple of those who had hesitated about making a choice turned to side them as they understood what was intended. The sudden storm was playing a part as well.

The rain come in a sweeping downpour; the half-light of the afternoon was blotted out as clouds rolled overhead. That gave the men who would not sell out a fighting chance. Not a good one, and against such odds as they faced, only two men managed to reach their horses. One of those was dead before he had ridden a dozen jumps, and he bounced loosely and tumbled to the ground again.

But the man who had led the defiance was getting away. North himself was shooting now, joining in the chase with frenzy in his voice. Most of the gun-hung crew that he had hired, renegades to start with, were trying to earn their money. But the one man was elusive as a dodging coyote. He reached the brush by the creek, and was swallowed by the lowering gloom.

It had looked like a short, quick storm, but now it held on with beating fury of rain until the real night came to take its place. Finally, soaked and disheveled, Medlow and half a dozen other men reported back at midnight, as the stars began to show again.

"We plumb lost his trail," Medlow said apologetically, "what with the rain and dark. But there's one thing sure. There was blood, every now and then. He's hit. So he won't get much farther."

"You blithering fool," North said bitingly. "You should have kept on till you got him! If he lives to tell of this—"

Medlow's face was sober.

"Don't forget that the rest of us are in this along with you," he reminded. "And we was workin' for Welch to start with. Anyhow, he'll be out to stop us in any case, for stealin' his herd. Ain't that what you hired a gun crew for?"

- 16 -

WELCH! North and Doll exchanged startled glances. Somehow it had not occurred to either of them that the man who was having this big herd gathered might be the father of Colin Welch. They had known that Colin was the son of a man from the North, but that meant little in itself. The despoilers of the land were as numerous, almost, as Yankee soldiers had been during the war years. And of the two, they were a far more rapacious species of locust.

One thing was certain. When all the bad news reached the ears of Welch, at the capital, he would be doubly bent on vengeance. That it would soon get back to him there was no doubt. Whether or not the wounded man survived to carry word, it would get there. Gathering distortion as it went, as the wind sweeps up dust.

They moved with the dawn, stirring the great herd to motion. There was one natural leader, a rawboned steer of considerable age and with a sweep of horn to match the spaces of Texas. He had lost one eye in a battle, but that was no handicap. Now he swung ahead, with all the showy confidence of the ignorant, and the rest fell in behind.

Yet it took over an hour to trail them out, such was the size of the herd. North viewed them calculatingly.

"Soon as we catch up with the first bunch, we'll split in two drives," he said. "They'll be big enough to handle that way."

Welch had provided a chuck wagon well laden with supplies. That would give two wagon loads of provisions— enough, as planned, for fifty men. For twice that number it would mean short rations during the worst weather of the winter.

That North appreciated how close they might be run was quickly demonstrated. On the second day at mid-morning he caught a man lunching as he rode, nibbling at a sandwich of biscuit and cold bacon. North pulled up.

"Where'd you get that?" he demanded.

"Outa the chuck wagon," he replied. "It was left over from breakfast—an' I like something to chew on."

"So do the rest of us," North said grimly. "And we'll be short enough before we reach the Arkansas. There'll be no more raiding the larder. Coffee at night when you're on duty, same as usual. Nothing more."

"Coffee," the luncher sneered. "You call that stuff we're drinkin' coffee? Tastes like warmed-over ditch water to me."

"Whatever it is, you'd better like it, for it's the best you'll get," North warned, and turned to ride on. But another word halted him.

"If that's the size of it—that we're goin' on half-rations now, an' starve before we get there, you can count me out at the start. I'll take my wages an' leave now."

North's eyes matched his name, but a fleck of angry red showed under the skin of his wind-burned cheeks.

"What's your name?" he demanded.

"Karth. Red Karth. from the Red River—"

"Then listen to me, Karth. Every man I hired was for the duration of the drive. Not to go one day, or a week or a month, but all the way. Didn't you understand that when you signed up?"

Karth shrugged, and tossed away the fatty portion of his chunk of bacon.

"Mebby I did," he conceded. "But I figured then it was a fair job with plenty to eat. Seems it ain't. And there's some other things developin' that I ain't partial to. So, as I say, I'll—"

Several others were within hearing now. North's voice crackled.

"You'll shut your mouth and do as you're told," he warned. "I'm holdin' every man to his agreement. Make no mistake about that!"

He swung again and rode off, and Karth made no rejoinder. Faces were thoughtful as the news spread. Rawe North was swinging a wide loop. But, while you might corral a lot of land and stock, it was something else again to hold captive the spirited and the unruly among men.

They passed the grave where two men were buried in nameless obscurity because they had placed honor above expediency—that grave where the herd had been driven across the new-made mound. Doll recognized it, though there was nothing now to indicate what it was. North rode past without a change of expression. Whether he noticed it or not Doll had no way of telling.

Farther on they encountered the other herd, drifting slowly, according to orders. Ames reported that there had been no trouble. But now, just ahead, was the saloon where North had gambled for the money with which he had bought Jim McLane's bunch. Garwood had furnished that money, however unwillingly. And Garwood, Doll guessed, would be waiting for them now.

Since towns of any sort would be few and far between, North allowed the crew to wash the dust from their throats here. It was a busy evening, but there was no sign of Garwood.

In the morning North issued fresh orders.

"We'll split the herd." he said. "Ames, you take half of them and go on ahead. We'll follow about half a day behind you. Doll, you'll rod this bunch. And now, as for the crews—"

He divided them up, an equal number to each bunch. They were in the midst of that task when the gun went off.

Ostensibly it was an accident. A gun fired through carelessness or mistake. Doll, swinging for a fast look, had his doubts on both scores, but there was no time then for speculation. Most of the crew were gathered at the one spot, and the big herd was rested and fractious again, their blood running hot with the excitement engendered of three herds too recently merged into one, of many minor battles which had ensued. It needed only the gun-shot to set them off, as though a trigger had been pulled.

Stampede! It was things like these which put spice in a cowboy's life and gray hairs in his head—if he lived long enough for his hair to gray. Such events kept many a man from ever growing old. Cattle were explosive as dynamite, unpredictable as the jump of a flea. Nothing suited them better than to choose a moment when everyone was off guard, then to run in a wild herd impulse, the massed rolling drive of a thundering juggernaut. Stampede!

Had they headed north it would have been simple. Let them run. But they were swinging east by south, and an hour now could mean a week's delay, the herd scattered and lost in the brush from which most of them had been so recently and painfully gathered. Later, farther north, where the land was open, with nothing in which to hide, it would be less of a chore to round them up again. Here it was stop them or lose them.

And to stop a stampede was akin to a man riding into a river and thinking thus to dam its flow to the sea. But they might, with luck, turn the vanguard, set the leaders to milling and so, in time, make a clockwise motion of the whole vast herd. No easy task, but one reckless to the point of folly. One which every cowboy faced as a part of the regular job at a moment's notice.

There was another, even more impelling reason for swinging them now. If allowed to run, the full weight of the herd would overwhelm the two chuck wagons, rolling them over, grinding down with the grim precision of the mills of the gods. If that happened, hunger indeed would ride north with them.

Doll had been on foot. He was in the saddle with a jump, leaning forward, gripping with his knees, shaking out the reins. No need, for the moment, to do more than that. His cayuse knew what to do at a time such as this as well as he did, was just as eager to do it. Give it its head and pray that it kept its feet.

North was racing beside him, as were Ames and Rowe and half a dozen others. Half a score against seven thousand. No time to look or choose now. You could only hope that there would be no hole or stone in the way to trip a horse. Now it was a solid mass of hoofs and horns coming at them, shaking the earth, sending up an enveloping cloud of dust. Keep running and pray for luck.

They were quartering to reach the tip of the wave which surged at them. Not led, this time, by the big steer with one eye. There was no leadership here, only flesh in the mass. Running at first in fear but with the sheer joy of deviltry aflame in wild blood. Running then in a terror generated of their own momentum, the wail of it rising in a wild bellow from thousands of throats. A bawl mounting and hoarse, such as might have come from the mouth of Paul Bunyan's great ox, causing the mountains to quake and tremble.

Here was the tip, the swing—if they could be made to swing. Doll's gun was in his hand, blasting at short range, while his horse ran warily, accommodating its speed to that of the cattle, keeping a jump away from reaching horns, yet close enough to squeal and bite and fight them to the turn.

North was using a bull-whip, a score of feet in length, heavy, savage in his hand. It popped like a pistol as it struck, and it could draw a furrow of blood across the nose of a cow or lift the eye out of a plunging steer. It twisted around a horn and broke it off. Men were yelling, screaming at the top of their voices, the sound swallowed like whispers. It was turn this mass now or be caught and ground beneath it.

But cool-headed experience was superior to wild running. Slowly the leaders were fought to a turn, and as they swung the movement spread to the packed herd behind. They were giving, beginning to mill. If nothing happened, they would miss the wagons.

Now they were turning, like a huge wheel. Bunches, a hundred head, two hundred, split off from sheer savage momentum and diverged, but the turn of the wheel was accelerating. It had been fast and hot—an hour that stretched like eternity and seemed only moments long. That was the way when it happened at all. Fast and hot and deadly, no time to think, to be afraid.

Now the leaders were eating the dust of the drag. The circle was complete. Men stopped screaming, as the wild bellow had ended in the throats of the herd. They spat black mud and wiped at reddened eyes which hardly showed from the crusted mask of dust and sweat. The herd was slowing.

The breath of horses was a hoarse sob. Cattle wheezed as they stumbled. Easy to hold them now, as men were detailed to ride guard. No more danger for a while. Not of that kind. But danger, on the trail, had a habit of striking when least expected, of a kind not counted on. It had been so this time, would be so again.

North was looking the men over, asking questions. With such a big crew it was not easy. But here was something— bone and blood and hide, where a steer had gone down and been tramped to pulp. Only a steer.

But farther on a rider lifted his hand in signal, then waited. What he had found was worse, for it was a man. His horse was not far off, in similar shape.

Only one man. Not a heavy toll, everything considered. But faces were a little grimmer as most of the crew gathered by the creek. Drinking, washing the crust from their faces. One man to bury. One man who had reached journey's end at its beginning.

North was silent while they washed and drank. The dust was settling now, a brown film everywhere. He worked the long bull-whip in his fingers, smoothing and coiling it. Then he spoke.

"Karth," step out!"

Karth hesitated, then shuffled forward, his face sullen.

"What do you want?" he demanded.

"It was your gun that fired that shot." North said. "And that shot started the stampede!"

Again Karth hesitated, as if about to make denial. Then he shrugged.

"What of it?" he challenged. "Accidents'll happen."

"Yeah, they'll happen," North agreed thinly. "But not that kind—not twice. One man is dead because of that. There might have been others. How did it happen?"

Some of the bravado was washed from Karth's face. He had admitted responsibility, and one man was dead. The look on the faces of the others was grim.

"I was lookin' at it, and my horse stumbled," Karth mumbled. "It just went off."

North's face was craggy, unpleasant. Doll felt no sympathy for Karth. He knew what was passing in North's mind, the same suspicion growing to certainty that was in his own. It had been no accident, that shot. He had been close to North at the moment, had heard the wild whine of the bullet. It had been a hasty shot and a wild one, but it had been intended to kill North.

That might be why Garwood had not showed up openly the night before. Easier to keep out of sight, to hire his killing done. Only he had picked a bungler to do the job.

But for the stampede, North would have killed Karth the next instant. Doll was sure of that. But there had been the stampede, a result of the shot unlooked for by Karth. And another man had died.

"I'm going to let you off easier than you deserve," North said. "Ames, you and a couple of the boys tie him to a wagon wheel. Take his shirt off. You've killed a man, and you might have killed others. You've lost us a couple hundred head of the herd—maybe more. You'll take a dozen lashes, Karth, and call yourself lucky."

They hesitated, but Ames stepped forward; others followed at his gesture. Karth retreated. He stopped with his back to the wagon, face twisting loosely. For a moment it looked as if he would try for his gun, but he was slow with a gun and his eyes were fixed on North, on the inexorable purpose in his face.

They tied him, stripping off his shirt. North lifted the whip, the tip wet and heavy already with the blood of cattle. It writhed out, and a red welt leaped across the white skin of Karth's back. A scream tore in his throat.

- 17 -

WHETHER that salutary lesson had been a good thing or not Doll was far from sure. He knew that this wasn't the way he would have handled it, but in these days there was no arguing with North. Always he had been a harsh man intent on his own way. Now he was ruthless.

Emlong, the grizzled little cook who had been with the big herd, was a man who possessed the know-how to dish up a meal and do it out of not much of anything, and still make it filling, almost satisfying. He had smeared grease across the back of Karth. Because he was in no shape to ride a horse, Karth was permitted to ride a chuck wagon and set to assisting Emlong and Sweeney, who had been with the other wagon.

Sweeney was big, slow-moving, slow of speech and thought. There was work enough for all three to feed that crew. Karth was a sick man, and subdued. So was the look on the faces of other men as they looked at him—subdued, speculative.

They had lost half a day, but luck had been with them. They gathered the herd without much loss, divided it and moved ahead. By the end of the second day they were again shaking down to the routine of the trail. One factor was in their favor. This was fall, and most drives headed up out of Texas in late winter or early spring. There would be no other herds to eat their graze or tangle with them.

But if that was in their favor, the winter itself would more than offset it. North was hoping for a mild and open winter. He counted on luck and enough grass along the way to push the herds through. But weather was as unpredictable as his own moods were becoming, and there were signs that the sea-

84

son would be early. The cattle had an unusually heavy coat, if that counted for anything. Old-timers insisted that it did.

There were other signs. Doll noted them, but he kept his own counsel. The tougher the ordeal the better, in his present mood. All that he wanted was hard work, long hours and weariness to the point where his mind could not keep on tormenting him. All of that he would get, he knew, but still he could not forget. He would start awake from a dream, and clench his fists as it dissolved to be only a dream. Altie!

Here was the Colorado, land of scrub oak and hackberry. Rolling country, with plenty of grass. But now the fall rains had started in earnest, and the days were short, the nights long and black. The wind which drove in their faces was raw with the breath of winter. Farther north—in Kansas, and on the far reaches of the Arkansas where they headed—the rain would be snow. If this kept up, it would soon be snow down here as well.

With provender short, the cooks were resorting principally to a stew. Emlong would slaughter a cow or steer, usually one that was lean and gaunt and showed no stamina to keep going. Its meat was lean and stringy, the steaks like whang-leather. Medlow chewed thoughtfully, slicing a chunk off with his bowie, and voiced the common thought.

"I've et a lot of vittles in my day—or stuff that passed for such," he grunted. "And plenty of steaks so tough you wondered was it meat or the sole of your boot with hob nails left in. But when you get gravy that bends the tines of a fork—that's going some!"

"Anyway, you can't say it don't stick to your ribs," big Sweeney said unsympathetically.

So mostly they made stew, heaping pots of it which was hot and flavorful, and by long boiling the meat could be chewed. Emlong was a genius at adding roots and herbs from along the way, and sometimes the result was good. Mostly the men didn't complain. There was enough else to gripe about, and when the sun did break through the clouds, on increasingly rare occasions, it seemed to have lost all warmth.

"Usually the air's alive with gnats an' bugs this time of year," Rowe observed reflectively. "Pester you savage. But this time it's too much for 'em."

Two things held them together. North, and his driving insistence that they press ahead. That, and the eagerness of most of them to get out of Texas. There could be plenty of trouble in the Nations, and no one had any illusions about all the long miles behind them.

There had been a well-marked trail at the start, a road pounded by countless hoofs where other herds had passed. Now there only was wild country. They were turning gradually west, partly because the grass was better, partly because their destination was different from that of most herds which swung up from Texas. West Kansas, where the Arkansas was young. Farther west than even North had ever gone before.

Doll knew his purpose. If men were ahead of them, waiting—as some assuredly would be—they would figure for them to follow the known trails. There was just a chance, in weather such as this, of fooling them by swinging well to the west.

Or so they had hoped. Until, with the Trinity in sight, riders came into sight behind them—full two score men as they counted, riding steadily. Most of these men wore the blue uniform of the army of the United States. The sun was out again, thin, without warmth. It glinted on rifles held across saddles.

No need to ask what that meant. Only one man in Texas, who was interested in them, would have the influence to send men of the army after them, or the grim purpose to do it. Welch.

Ames and the first herd was on ahead, nearly to the river. But still in sight, a vast brown blotch which crawled over the earth. North had been up there with them. He came back down, rode beside Doll.

"What do you make of it?" he asked.

"Looks like trouble," Doll said. "It's the law—such law as they have in Texas these days. And they figure they've the force to back it up."

"Likely," North agreed. He appeared unworried. "Well, we'll see!"

Doll looked at him, startled.

"Anything we do, it'll be wrong," he warned.

"We'll see," said North again.

Doll was puzzled. This was a strange reaction on North's part. The men in blue were coming up now, led by a captain.

Men who had been traveling light and fast. There was a look about them of men who expected trouble and knew what to do with it.

"Tell the boys to keep on with what they're doing." North instructed. "We'll act as if we didn't know what this was all about."

The soldiers pulled to a halt, keeping in formation, at ease but ready for anything. The captain rode forward stiffly.

"I'm looking for a man named North," he said. "Redding is my name."

He dismounted, with the stiffness of a man overlong in the saddle. He was short and wide, and walked assertively, coming down hard on the heels. His eye was cold.

"I'm North." North conceded. "Glad to know you, Captain Redding. What's on your mind?"

Redding wasted no words.

"We are here as the law," he said. "We represent, at the moment, the state of Texas."

He threw that out like a challenge, but North did not pick it up.

"That so?" he asked. "If there's any information I can give you, I'll be glad to. But I doubt if we'll be able to help you. We've seen no fugitives along the way."

"We're here at the instigation of a man named Welch," Redding grunted. "That mean anything to you?"

"Welch?" North stroked his chin. "Welch?" he repeated. "Yes, now I remember. There was a man of that name at Longhorn. He and a friend of his tried to kill Mr. Doll and myself. It was an unprovoked attack, and they shot first. Surely such an affair has not brought a detachment of the army way out here?"

"So that's what happened to the young'un," Redding shrugged. "No, it's his father that I'm referring to. He says that you stole his herd."

If he felt any apprehension at what might lie ahead, face to face with two crews, both of which would outnumber his own men, he was hiding it under this aggressive cloak of bluntness. But North seemed more puzzled than ever.

"Stole his herd?" he repeated. "I'm afraid I don't understand you."

Redding waved a pudgy hand.

87

"You've got a lot of cattle here," he pointed out. "And plenty of them, or so he claims, had been gathered by order of Welch. One of his men, as it happens, told how you took them. He lived long enough to give details," he added drily.

Doll saw the quick gleam in North's eyes which that incautious revelation drew. So the man who had got away was dead. That meant that there was no witness left alive.

He turned, and saw Karth watching them from the shelter of the nearer wagon. Watching with avid eyes. Doll strolled toward the wagon.

"That's all most interesting, Captain," North conceded. "I knew I had enemies in this country. But I didn't suppose that anyone would go to such lengths to make up a story so ridiculous on the face of it."

Emlong, within the wagon, glanced at Doll, then shifted his gaze to Karth.

"Get to peelin' spuds," he ordered. "He'll not interfere," he added to Doll. "I'll see to that."

Nodding, Doll strolled back. Redding was teetering back and forth on the balls of his feet.

"Ridiculous, is it?" he demanded. "That's a matter of opinion."

North shrugged.

"Opinions don't cut much ice," he said bluntly. "Though of course you're welcome to your own."

"If you didn't steal 'em, where'd you get a herd of this size?" Redding demanded. "It looks to be about the size of that bunch that had been gathered for Welch. Likewise there's a lot of brands represented."

"Naturally there's a lot of brands," North agreed. "Show me any big herd in Texas that's all one brand where they have any. As for the size of it, I've got another bunch of equal number, up ahead there. Seven thousand head in all. As to where I got them—where would you suppose? I came to Texas to buy cattle, as I've done before. I bought them."

A faint smile of incredulity crossed the face of the lieutenant who stood behind Redding.

"Bought them, eh?" the captain repeated. "I'd like to see the proof of that—or is that just a matter of opinion, too? You'd have a bill of sale from Colin Welch, maybe?"

Up to now, North had held his temper admirably. Now he grew tough in turn.

"I would not," he retorted. "Just because Colin Welch may have lost some cattle don't mean that I've got them. From what I've heard since I came to Texas, Welch is a damned carpet-bagger, and so I'm not surprised. Probably he's sold them himself and is tryin' a double-cross on whoever owned them, sayin' they were stolen so as to get out of paying for them. It's about what I'd expect. But I don't do business with men like Welch."

Redding scowled.

"Callin' men like him names won't get you anywhere," he warned. "And what I want is proof—"

"I'll call men like him any name I like, either to you or to their face, if I ever get a chance," North said flatly. "I don't like to be called a cattle-thief, and particularly by a man of his stripe. As to proof—I do have a bill of sale. Not from a man such as Welch, but a man who's known all over Texas. And known as an honest man. Here, take a look. Here's the bill of sale for seven thousand head."

He pulled a long red leather purse from his pocket, extracted a folded slip of paper and held it out. Doll recognized it. It was the bill of sale which Jim McLane had given them when North had bought the thousand head from him.

But that had been for a thousand head. Doll looked closer, as Redding unfolded it. He remembered now that North had written that bill of sale in advance. For one thousand head of cattle, at a price of three thousand dollars.

Now he understood why North had been so anxious to buy and pay cash for the thousand head, purchasing them from a a man so well known as Jim McLane, making sure that there was nothing even remotely crooked about the whole deal. He had Jim McLane's signature on the bill of sale, the sign of an honest man.

But some time since then North had made two slight changes in the paper, minor ones which none the less altered it considerably. The top of the figure one had been crossed, changing it to a seven. A nought had been added after the figure three. Now it read seven thousand head, purchased for a price of thirty thousand dollars.

CAPTAIN REDDING perused the paper carefully. He turned then for a long look at the herds, and shrugged with the weariness of a man who has followed a false lead to a futile conclusion.

"This seems to be in order," he conceded. "Also I have the honor to be acquainted with Jim McLane. His signature is as distinctive as himself—Light of Mars—and there is no question in my mind but what this is genuine. Sorry to have troubled you, Mr. North."

"I expect that the trouble has been mostly the other way around," North suggested, eyeing the tired troopers. "Won't you and your men spend the night with us and sample our beef stew?"

"You tempt me, sir—tempt me strongly," Redding confessed. "But I'm afraid we'd better be starting back. A good day to you, Mr. North."

Laughter boomed deep in North's throat. A rare mirth, for him. The soldiers were vanishing in the distance, and he waved one hand in mocking salute.

"Tough luck, boys," he sympathized. "To ride all this way and then find a bill of sale signed by Old Man Texas himself! I suspect that our captain knows there's something wrong about the deal, but it lets him out, and he wasn't too anxious for trouble on a carpet-bagger's account. By the time Jim McLane can be consulted, we'll be out of Texas."

That was true, but there was wild land beyond Texas, and neither a river nor a shadowy border-line would hold back vengeance. But North's gamble had paid off. Once across the Red, they would be beyond law or even the pretense of it.

They crossed the Trinity. It had not been affected by the rains, and there was no trouble. But the cattle were sullen, like the weather. Mile on endless mile they plodded each day while the gray light lasted. Mud and cold and broken sleep at night for the men. Every living creature was ganting up, drawn fine and hard, but drawing already on reserves of fat and stamina.

Moving along as they must, the cattle could not get quite enough to eat. It was the same with the men, for a different reason. There was little enough dry wood for cooking. Seldom did luck go with them to the point of finding enough for a roaring bonfire at which to dry and warm themselves.

Then a quickening beat of excitement. The Red was ahead, a distant gleam in a flash of sunshine. Both were welcome. And, so far, there had been no real trouble.

Maybe they had outguessed their foes. It was a chance, but Doll put no faith in it. If his hunch was right, there'd be trouble waiting at the Red. Vengeance, while they were still in Texas.

But trouble again came from behind. Not in a threatening guise, this time. It was a lone horseman who had followed the trail, a man who rode slumped in the saddle, his face gray as the weather. Doll saw him first, and called North. They watched his approach, puzzled.

"Now what'd an old-timer like him be doing, off by his lonesome at this time of year?" North wondered aloud.

"Maybe that's Pleasant, catchin' up with his herd," Doll suggested.

North gave him a startled look. It was idle speculation on Doll's part, and no one was more surprised than he when the oldster came up and confirmed it.

"Howdy!" he greeted, and moved stiffly in the saddle. "Ouch!" A strained smile overspread his face. "My name's Pleasant, but weather like this an' all, I'm havin' me a gosh-durned hard time to live up to it!"

It required only a look to see that the man was ill. He should have been in a warm bed with the comforts of civilization around him, instead of riding a winter trail. His turkey looked like an under-fed bird of the same name. Doll glanced at North, and saw the strain on his face. Pleasant, unnoticing, continued cheerfully.

"Reckon it won't be the effort to do it tonight, at that," he added. "I've been alone, ridin', ridin', ridin' for a right long spell, seems like, and a man gets a hankerin' for comp'ny. Been travelin' to ketch up with a bunch of cattle I got somewhere along the trail."

"In that case, you can rest easy," North returned. "You've found them."

91

"Found them? Eh?" Pleasant twisted to gaze with rheumy eyes at the big herd, at the distant blotch of the second bunch up ahead, with the river beyond it. "You mean—?"

"We caught up with your bunch, and now we're all travelin' together," North explained. "We figured it would make it easier, all around. Our route is for my ranch in the western part of Kansas. That's about where you wanted to go, isn't it?"

"Why—why yes, I guess mebby 't is." Surprise held Pleasant speechless for a moment. "I was gettin' my hopes up when I first saw a herd ahead," he confessed. "Then I figured I was sure wrong. Too big to be mine. But—that news sure does brighten things up, like'n if the sun was bustin' through them clouds. B'golly, yes."

North blew his nose, loudly. His usually craggy face had lost some of its contours.

"My name's North," he explained. "And this is Noland Doll. Come along up to the chuck wagons—one of them belongs to you, anyway. We'll be camping for the night, and you look as if you could use a good feed."

"Sure can. M' turkey's about flat. Mighty glad to meet you, North. An' you, son. Golly, I can't get over this. Be a lot nicer, 's you say, to travel 'long together this way. Guess I'm gettin' kinda old. Weather makes m' old bones creak."

He was garrulous, a flush of excited color in the gray of his cheeks as they approached the wagons. He dismounted, so stiff that he staggered and all but fell. Doll caught his arm, and he smiled apologetically.

"Guess I ain't just myself, son," he sighed. "Kinda had some tough luck, down where I used t' live. Lost Ma last winter—then other things went wrong. Took the truck out of me when Ma went. We'd aimed to make a new start, up north som'ers, and so I knew Ma'd want me to go on anyway, like we'd planned. Guess I was a mite late, gettin' started."

The news was spreading as the cowboys came in for chuck. For the most part they were silent and grim. They knew the story of this herd, and by now they knew North, or thought they did. Doll caught a muttered growl or so.

"Me, I can go for a lot. But this sticks in my craw. If the boss was to kill the old geezer at the start, it wouldn't be so bad as playin' with him this way! I sure as hell don't like it."

To their surprise, as well as Doll's, North himself materialized out of the shadows. His voice was edged.

"Reckon mebby I've got that comin'," he acknowledged. "But you're draggin' your loop too wide when you think I'm playin' with the old man. His herd belongs to him—and all the range he needs to run them on, when we get there! I didn't know he wasn't another Welch!"

They stared at him, astonished at this new revelation, as North moved away again. Doll felt warmed. Hard, North might be and was, a man to fit his environment, without scruple. But he had his points. Pleasant could ride in the chuck wagon now, and sleep in peace.

With the morning it was apparent that he would have to travel in that fashion for a while. He had kept going on sheer nerve, but now that the necessity for it was past, the let-down was marked. Pleasant was a sick man. He protested at being babied, insisted that he should ride with the rest of them, but subsided when North insisted that he not only ride in his own wagon, but that he stay in bed for a day or so as they journeyed.

Emlong, at North's suggestion, gathered sage and other herbs and mixed a potent brew with which to dose the sick man. Doll sniffed it as it boiled and shook his head.

"That stuff ought to kill or cure," he said. "It's make me sick just to take it."

"I've brung more'n one feller onto his feet with that tea," Emlong insisted. "Ain't nothin' bad about it but the taste. It's a mite on the strong side, I'll admit. But I've took it myself."

North was moody and silent. They rode ahead to join the lead bunch as they neared the river. Luck was with them. This was low water season, and though they had traveled by guess in a trailless land, a good crossing lay ahead. One unmarked by any tracks of man or beast.

"We'll bring both bunches up close and cross in the morning," North decided. "What do you think of it?"

Doll shook his head.

"I don't like it," he confessed. "I doubt if Welch would put all his trust in the army. And then there's Garwood.

who's never made a move—yet. And this is the edge of Texas."

"That's the way I feel," North agreed. "It looks too good. You and me will take us a ride—after dark."

Doll knew what he had in mind. If Pleasant could find them, so might others. This was the Red. If they were to be stopped at all, here was the place. Absence of any sign was more suspicious now than mark of it would have been.

There was no moon. Clouds had spread in a creeping haze as the dark closed down. They rode upstream for a couple of miles, their horses picking their way in the heavy gloom. It would rain again before morning. and the prospects were not cheerful. Back at camp there was fresh grumbling. Muted protests which would swell to a growl as the miles dragged out behind.

Unable to see more than the dark sheen of the water, they had to chance it when they turned to cross. Luck did not favor them, for almost at once the horses were swimming. The bite of the water was savage with winter. Doll clenched his teeth and took it as icy waves lapped high. They reached the far shore and the horses struggled out, shaking themselves. Here they could only ride in silence. The cayuses could keep their blood astir by moving, but even that was denied them.

Here were bluffs, broken country which would afford plenty of hiding places—and excellent opportunity for an ambush as the herd started across. Maybe nothing like that was waiting. But the lack of it would surprise Doll more than the presence.

The wind was blowing, and it cut through sodden clothes as spear-tipped horn would rip. Nothing showed in the gloom. They swung and quartered back from the river, and both men were beginning to wonder if they had been wrong, when they saw a gleam like a low-hung star. But the clouds had long since blotted away all stars.

"Campfire," North said. "You go have a look. It'll give you a chance to stir around."

One of them had to stay with the horses. Doll worked closer, on foot. The ground was frozen under his feet, no longer spongy. Even the exercise could not warm him. Then the fire showed bright as he looked down at it, envious of its heat. Men lolled about, or lay rolled in blankets beyond. Many men.

"Better get some sleep, I guess," one of those by the fire yawned. "They'll be startin' to cross, come daylight, and we've got to be ready for them."

"How many do you figure?" another man inquired.

"Close to a hundred, I'd say. But we've got forty, and that's plenty. Wait till they're in the middle of the river, then start pickin' 'em off, get the herd to milling. By the second volley the odds'll favor us."

"I'd take them on if it was ten to one," a third man growled. "That herd'll never leave Texas—not while they drive them!"

Doll had heard enough. Forty men, set to ambush them as they came. Their hunch had been right. He returned to where North waited, and they crossed back to the Texas shore and a few hours of sleep. But long before daylight Doll was in the saddle again, this time with thirty men behind him.

"I'll stick with the cattle," North explained. "We'll have to start across as they expect. Wait till they start something —then wipe them out!"

I was to be what the others planned, but in reverse. An ambush for the 'bushers. Those who planned to sow the wind would reap a bitter hurricane.

- 19 -

SOUND FLOWED above the uneasy suck and gurgle of the river—a swelling turbulence which denoted that the big herds were being pushed into the muddying edge of the Red. Doll, straining his eyes in the half-light of dawn, could see the dim mass of them a mile away. He felt the water in his boots, cold as ice. Pulsing blood seemed to have no power to warm the white flesh at a man's extremities. It was bad now, it would be worse as winter closed about them. Meanwhile there was work to do.

Half a mile back from the water they found their enemies' remuda, with two men guarding the cayuses. Men who looked impatiently toward the south, ears cocked for the first sound of the guns. Resentful men who wanted to be in at the fight, who had no inkling that trouble would come this far to seek them.

One turned to stare into the round bore of a revolver close to his eyes. His hands jerked like the beating wings of a captive hawk. The other man was of sterner stuff. His eyes widened, and then he was trying for his gun, starting to throw himself down behind the shelter of a boulder. Doll swept his horse alongside, his own revolver chopped down in a hammerstroke. Shapeless hat and unkempt thatch of hair dulled the thud of it, but the running man stumbled and sank to his knees, and the half drawn gun slid and made a little furrow in the sand.

"Take their guns," Doll ordered his men. "That's enough. If they want to run, let them. Texas is big."

He set two men in turn to watch the horses, hazing them to a new hiding place. Then he led the way, coming up from behind to where a line of watchers would be crouched. Doll dismounted, and the others followed his example, not waiting to be told. Each man knew his job, without the need of words.

They moved on foot, the river again in sight, a dull gray sheen in the dawn. One man blew softly on numbed fingers. There was a dank mist rising from the water, a chill wind beginning another day. The hot coffee they had swallowed an hour before was only a memory. There was no warmth anywhere, even deep inside a man.

Doll had already picked the most likely spot for the ambush. A long, low ridge, running a litle distance back from the river and parallel with it, an embankment from which guns could rake the crossing herd and those who came with it. A place made to order for massacre.

He saw the back of a crouching man, and another beyond him. The herd was a formless wedge in the half-light, crowding deep into the river. Light glinted along raised gun barrels. Doll lifted his own revolver and fired a quick shot over the heads of the men on the ridge.

A rifle went off like an echo. Probably it was a nervous finger on the trigger, acting in gesture purely involuntary. But it was enough to make nerves jump, to swing the line of them around with guns raising.

Doll had hoped to do this without a battle, to warn this bunch and disarm them. That wouldn't please North, who had ordered that they be wiped out. But Doll had been thinking of Altie. Altie, with flame in her hair, and an unexpected tenderness of heart. He felt that she would approve his way.

Now there was no time for thinking. Only it wasn't going to work like that.

A man beside him coughed and slumped to the ground. Red flamed from gun muzzles, and it was folly to stand up and shoot back, but he was running as he had done in the old war days, shouting, leading his men. They had called him Major Doll then. Before that charge the line ahead wavered and broke.

Most of them. Not all. A big man was standing there, like a deep-rooted tree, feet wide apart, brushing the hair back from his eyes with impatient gesture. There was something familiar about him, and suddenly Doll knew what it was. It seemed to transport him back to that saloon called the Paddle Wheel, so that he was facing Colin Welch again.

Only this was an older man, and there was vague regret in him that it had to be this way. He shot from the hip, and felt the twitch of the other man's bullet through his hat, saw a lock of hair sheared off. His own hair. That had been close.

But Welch was down, and his men were retreating, shooting as they could, dodging for cover. Unable to return to their horses, realizing belatedly that they could not reach them again. The knowledge that they were being squeezed between the closing jaws of a trap made them more deadly. They fought back doggedly, and finally a score of them reached the river and plunged in. Some of them would get across to hide in the brush and brakes along the Texas shore.

Doll left the harrying of them to others. He was suddenly sick of it all, and whatever happened, this particular crew would bother them no more. Those who survived the river and the man-hunt would be fully occupied with the effort to keep alive, to get back to food and shelter, stumbling along on foot, with winter pressing them hard.

But maybe they were lucky. They were heading south, not north into the teeth of winter. North's crew should have been jubilant in the face of so easy and complete a victory.

Instead, they paused to dig a few graves, then went on again with storm beating in their faces. Rain, driving pellets with the wind behind it, was soaking them anew as day came, fulfilling the grim promise of the night.

The cattle were restive. They strove constantly to get off by themselves, singly or in bunches, to stop and stand while the others drifted past. They would get worse as the trail lengthened. Instead of following, the riders must harry them, constantly watchful. Most of the danger of stampede, always present by spring and summer, was gone in this weather. But these conditions were worse. The one good thing about it was that it kept men occupied, and effort helped warm sluggish blood.

Pleasant still rode in his own chuck wagon. He lay swathed in blankets, dutifully drinking the bitter concoction which Emlong served up, protesting that he should be riding with the others, doing his share of the work. But his protests were feeble. He was a sick man, scarcely able to raise his head.

"No wonder North didn't battle him," Karth grunted. "He could see, plain enough, that Pleasant'd never live long. If there'd been a chance he could, it'd have been a different story."

"Some day," Emlong warned, "you're goin' to shoot off that mouth a' your'n once too often, Karth. When you do—smearin' grease on yore back won't help none."

It was a wild land now through which they struggled, and desolate. The Nations. Forbidden territory by the laws of either white man or red. Here a dozen tribes prowled, quarreling among themselves, but all united and fiercely vindictive against the whites. But at this season the cowboys saw no sign of hostiles as they penetrated deeper into this storm-swept wilderness. Spring and summer was the time for fighting. Winter a time for huddling in well banked tepees against the cold. North had counted on that in making his plans.

Overnight the rain turned to snow. The land brown and sere at dusk, was white in the dawn, so that the horizon was false, the sky closing above them like a weight. Yet there was no relief in the change. The snow was wet, sodden, melting on man and beast, the wind relentless and unyielding. Cook-fires at the lee of the wagons smoked and spluttered, and the cooks were hard put to it to serve up hot food. There was nothing else hot in this cold land. No warm place anywhere. It seemed to Doll that he had never been warm.

No man had shaved since leaving Texas. They looked shaggy as bears, and their tempers matched their looks. Winter was definitely upon them now. The snow had ceased to be wet, but even that was something to look back to with regret. At least it had been warm enough for it to melt. Now it was hard and flinty, and getting so deep that the cattle had difficulty in finding grass.

"I seem to be having the devil's own luck," North growled. "This is the earliest snow, this far south, that I've ever seen or heard tell of. If it keeps up this way—"

He left the sentence unfinished, but Doll needed no elaboration. Unless they had better weather, the cattle would starve. And so would the men. Supplies were running dangerously short. Not only were they traveling slower than they had counted on, but it seemed that everything was against them.

"We'll get fresh supplies as soon as we cross the Canadian," North promised. "There's a trading post back in there—run by a man name of McQueen. He's been on the good side of the Indians—had to be, of course, to live there. And most of his customers have been outlaws, men who've hid out in the Nations and beyond. But he'll sell to us, and we'll be in fine shape then."

That promise was like a beacon. Doll suspected that it was all that held them together as an unwieldy crew. But for the hope of it, many of them would have risked North's wrath and the dangers of the trail behind to turn back. But if there was food ahead, that was what they wanted. What they must have.

"Reckon a man can keep alive on stew an' beefsteak," Rowe commented distastefully. "Anyway, we're doing it. But ef'n I ever get to the place where I don't *have* to eat stew, I reckon I'd be plumb likely to murder a man that suggested it to me."

Which seemed to pretty well sum up the feeling of all of them. Pleasant alone did not complain. He was no better, but he hung onto the thin thread of life like a spider to its web. Even Karth grudgingly admitted that North was doing all he could for the sick man. He visited with him two or three times a day, discussing plans for the ranch Pleasant would have alongside his own spread in Kansas. North painted a picture which glowed brighter by contrast with the conditions surrounding them, and Doll suspected that it was all that kept Pleasant alive.

They sighted the Canadian. Ordinarily it was a turbulent stream and a dread name to men driving a trail herd. Here it looked peaceful but cold. Ice fringed either shore, but the water was clear and shallow. There seemed no likelihood of trouble as they started across.

Long since the two herds had been merged again as one. It was easier to keep one bunch on the move in such weather, requiring fewer men for night duty. Even so, animals and men alike stumbled with weariness, and it was that factor which added up to near-disaster at mid-river. A cow stumbled and went down, and her hoarse bawl of terror and despair set those close at hand to milling in blind panic. In a matter of seconds it had infected half the herd.

Normally, even then, it would not have been bad. The river was not deep nor swift enough to bother much. But the wagons had started across, a little way down-stream. All at once the wave of the herd was surging, threatening to engulf them.

Emlong yelled at his team, though they needed no urging. The wiry cayuses knew their peril as well as he did. A wagon could be overturned in such a melee, and then, caught in the middle of a milling jam, man or horses would be helpless. Behind the seat Pleasant half raised up in his blankets, conscious that something out of the ordinary was happening.

One horse, plunging wildly, went off into a deep hole. The next instant the wagon overturned, spilling on its side.

North was the closest of the men on horseback. He spurred hard, forcing his horse toward the melee, reckless of the menace still exploding out from the packed mass of the herd upstream. He saw Emlong working to get the team on their feet again, hopeless as that seemed with the wagon dragging at them. But back in that confusion of canvas and box was Pleasant, trapped and helpless.

The milling mass of the herd was around him now, horns raking wildly, hoofs churning. Emlong did the only thing he could, as one horse kicked itself loose from the harness. He caught it and managed to get on its back. It was still touch and go whether the cayuse could keep its feet and save itself and its rider. The wagon and the supplies it contained were hopelessly lost.

North had a knife out, the blade opened. He slashed at the dragging canvas, ripped a slice of it away. Then he grabbed, and had Pleasant in his grasp, still wrapped mummy-like in the now sodden blankets. A heave of the lurching wagon, with cattle crowding it hard, almost sent it toppling over him, but his horse backed away, biting viciously at the animals in its path. North clutched his burden in front of him.

Other riders were driving in among the milling herd, beating them into a semblance of order again. North's cayuse plunged through a red sea of heaving backs and thrusting horns, then there was open water. He reached the shore, rode to where the other wagon was drawn up, and stripped the icy blankets off Pleasant. Karth, working to start a fire, stared curiously at the now pallid face of the invalid.

"Looks like he was near finished, this time," he said. "You won't have to share with him."

"Get that fire going, damn you," North ordered. "Bring some dry blankets, and jump! We'll get him warm—get him to McQueen's. Mebby that'll help him."

Karth backed away, tripped, and sprawled headlong. But he was up again like a scared rabbit at the look in North's face, grabbing wildly for blankets, scuttling to use their last precious bunch of dry wood to feed the blaze along.

- 20 -

McQUEEN's! That was the slogan now. To reach the trading post, there to get help for Pleasant, to obtain fresh supplies. With only one wagon left and half their scanty stock of food gone in the hungry maw of the Canadian, it had become doubly necessary now. McQueen's was like a lodestar on the long trail to the Arkansas.

No one, not even North, knew exactly where McQueen's was located. Somewhere back in these wild brakes, on a tributary of the river. And not far ahead now—two or three days, maybe a week. Not far as miles went.

Wolves skulked openly on the outskirts of the big herd, waiting to pull down stragglers, to feast on the weak. They grew daily more bold, keeping just beyond the line of accurate gun-fire by day, coming in close at night. Men, riding night-guard, would see green eyes which blazed and faded only to reappear again not far off. Their ghostly serenade had a savage quality to it.

Two days later, Karth disappeared. With him went a horse and a sack of desperately needed supplies. North called Ames.

"Take two men," he instructed. "Trail him—to hell, if necessary. Bring him back—or kill him!"

"He won't be brought back alive—not after what happened last time," Rowe prophesied, watching his friend ride away. "Leastways, I wouldn't—not if I was him."

Pleasant was still alive. That was about all that could be said for him. He lay now, mostly silent, uncomplaining, a wraith of a man. He had been shaken by chills, following that immersion in the river, until, as Emlong complained, he shook the wagon. It had taken a long time to get him warm again. Even now he didn't look warm. Warmth was something to dream about, but never quite to attain.

North worked harder to keep a spark of life in Pleasant than he had ever done for himself or to move the herd. He seemed to have centered all his will here, that Pleasant should live. Some found it incomprehensible.

"If Pleasant dies, North'll have his herd back, just like that," one man muttered. "And he stole it in the first place—"

"He didn't know the shape Pleasant was in," Doll explained. "He'll fight a man that's able to hit back, and give no quarter. But he'd give up half the herd to put the old man on his feet again, and do it without turnin' a hair."

It was this quality in North, perhaps, which Marian Breen had sensed and liked. Because of it, Doll had sided him where otherwise he would have pulled back. But unless they found this place called McQueen's, it was not alone Pleasant who would be in bad shape.

North had grown increasingly silent. He rode aloof from

the rest of them, and what his thoughts might be they could only conjecture. Only he talked to Pleasant—talked like a son, and joked. With the rest of them he was driving, always driving—men and horses and cattle alike. He was tireless, possessed of a rocky endurance to match his face. But the land was empty before them.

That emptiness was the worst. The cold and the snow could be endured. But now it seemed as though they had left all of life behind. Even the sun, symbol of warmth, was remote and becoming more so. This might be a near-paradise by summer. It was wasteland by winter.

There was no sign of Ames nor the men who had gone with him. The ever moving wind wiped away tracks in a matter of minutes, or hours at most. Where Karth traveled it was like following a wraith, and where this town of Mc-Queen's might be was equally hard to guess. Until, all at once, the sun came out dazzlingly white across the snow, and they saw it ahead.

For a moment even Doll doubted his eyes, wondering if it was some sort of a mirage. A low ridge of hills reared just short of the horizon, and several buildings, mostly 'dobe, clustered at their foot. This would be McQueen's. It could be nothing else.

Even the cattle seemed to catch the pulse of excitement. They pressed ahead with new interest, and it was not until they were nearing the place that fresh misgivings smote the men. No smoke arose from any chimney. Nor was there a break in the unbroken snow along the single street.

North fought down a feeling close to panic. This was Mc-Queen's. It answered the description he had heard of the place, and there was no other town or trading post in all this whole section of wilderness. But that something was wrong was doubly evident as a coyote slunk away at their approach.

The buildings had an air of having been lived in, and not long before. Neither dust nor desertion had left a settled imprint. But they contained only emptiness now. And in the main building, the store, there was a note waiting for them —lying on the counter, boldly written.

"You're too late, North. Now you can starve—and freeze! But they say it's warm in hell!"

That was all. North stared at it with burning eyes, swept

his gaze across the bare shelves. Emptiness! They had crossed the Red, had beaten off attack, had plodded the endless miles against mounting odds. But here, where he had least expected it, enemies had been ahead of them, had won a bloodless but decisive battle.

McQueen of course had been persuaded to sell out, for a price. A renegade to start with, such an act was in keeping with his character. The emptiness of the place testified to it. Every man who had habited the town had departed, and they had taken everything which might be useful. There was no food on the shelves of the store, nothing to sustain life. What had been here might be cached a mile away, or a hundred. There was no track in the shifting snow, no way of telling.

A thorough search failed to reveal anything which they could use. North looked at the bleak, dismayed faces of his crew, and gestured.

"They sold out," he said shortly. "They think they've got us licked, but we'll fool them. We'll live without their help. But when the rats that have nested here get ready to come back—they can have some of their own medicine. Burn what you can and smash the rest."

In that hour, North was a leader. Somehow he infused his own spirit into the men. They were almost jaunty in their defiance as they went on.

It was the next day that the blizzard struck. This was a norther—a true blizzard, sweeping down from Canada, gaining in ferocity as it marched. It began with a keening wind and blinding snow, and soon the storm had shut away the herd so that each man found himself alone in a world of choking white. As it increased the air grew colder, until, despite all that could be done, the big herd was turning tail, drifting with the storm, and men could only follow, taking such care as they were able that not too many should be lost, where to stop moving meant to freeze.

For twenty-four hours there was no lessening in the fury. Eighteen inches of fresh snow fell, and now starvation faced the herd as it did the men. Hunger and cold. Then it cleared, and here was a new and worse hazard, aftermath of the storm.

Driving continually, the snow had crusted heavily on the

backs of every animal. Now they saw that it had done more than that. It was across their faces as well. an icy sheath which crusted closed eyes. The herd, still stumbling along uncertainly, was blind.

Here was an added job for men so bone-weary that they could hardly keep going. Unable to see, the cattle did not sheer off at their approach. But it was a formidable job to seek out cow after cow, to rap them sharply across the head a time or so and crack that mask of ice loose. Yet it had to be done.

Probably it was hopeless. The snow was too deep now for them to find grass, save where the wind had swept it aside, piling huge drifts at the expense of these barren stretches. Drifts in which faltering stock would plunge and then stand helplessly to freeze if men were not constantly on guard to prevent it and to pull them loose.

But there was nothing to do but point them into the northwest again and keep moving. Keep moving till they died. There was nothing else to do, nowhere else to go. Even those who hated North knew that their only salvation lay in sticking with him. He'd bring them through, or they'd all die together.

"Two days," Emlong grunted, and fumbled icicles from his mustache and sent the ice shivering against his dying fire. "Two days, and we'll scrape the bottom of the barrel. Nothin' left then but stew, an' nothin' in the stew but beef—if you can call them bones beef."

"Two days is as long as they'll be able to stagger without more grass than they're getting," Doll retorted grimly. "So the one evens the other."

"Yeah." Emlong climbed into the wagon, shaking his head. Then he stuck it out again, his voice raspy with an added gruffness.

"One man's lucky," he said. "Pleasant. He's gone on to greener pastures."

- 21 -

THEY managed a shallow grave, there in the frozen wastes. With a big flat stone which it took three men to move, to lay above it. That would serve as a marker, would keep the wolves away. It was an unlooked-for ending, this concern for a man from whom North had originally stolen a herd.

But there could be no doubt in any man's mind now that Pleasant had touched the one soft spot in their employer. He helped with the digging, and from somewhere he dug out a dog-eared Bible and read a few words while the wind whistled its own dirge and the dark closed down again. And tears closed on his cheeks.

"Dust to dust," North said, and closed the book. "But he was named right. Pleasant. . . . I never knew my own folks. If I'd known my father—and if he'd been a man like him—"

He left the thought abruptly unfinished, turning away, but men understood. With the dawn, however, bones seemed to creak like the ungreased wheels of the wagon. Discouragement was in every man, every beast. One of the crew voiced it dully, looking down at the new-made grave, already one with the rest of the land in the drifting snow.

"Reckon he's lucky," he said. "Most of us won't get that much—or a stone to keep the wolves from feastin'."

North, swinging heavily into his saddle, faced around at that.

"Who's talkin' of dying?" he asked harshly. "This is no land for quitters—and we're not quitting! Storm, or cold, or the devil himself can't stop us here! We'll reach Kansas! Make no mistake about it! When the grass grows green, we'll be there with it!"

Somehow he goaded them to movement. One plodding foot in front of another, as the hours dragged by. Agony for man and beast. It came up from the throats in a tortured lowing, like a dirge. But they moved—moved to keep from freezing where they stood, and they moved north toward Kansas.

At mid-day, as though the fates relented, they came across a man. The storm had closed around them again, thick and blanketing, so that he rode among them before he was aware that they were there. The wind had swept away the sound of the bawling herd, for he rode with it where they faced its cutting edge. And a heavy scarf tied over his ears further blanketed them.

Doll saw him first, but North was beside him as the man

106

stared out of glazing eyes and tried belatedly to swing. North caught him, heavy fingers closing crab-like on a shoulder, wrenching the man around. One who rode with well fed look to him.

"What's the hurry, stranger?" North demanded. And then: "Who might you be?"

It was the terror, so plain to read in this man's face, which told him more than the jerky words.

"Why, I—I'm Cowan. I—"

North reached then, his own hand unmittened, and jerked away cap and muffling scarf, revealing the bright carroty red of the newcomer's hair. His voice, surprisingly, was a chuckle, but utterly without mirth.

"Cowan, eh? That'll do to tell tenderfeet. I've heard too much of that red head of yours, McQueen."

They dragged him inside the wagon, where the wind was shut away. The fear in McQueen was understandable then, knowing who he was. But now he was regaining control of himself.

"They took my store and turned me out," he whined. "Kicked me out of my own post at gun-point! I tried to find somebody to help me against them, and I couldn't. Then I remembered that you might be comin', like they said, and I turned back. I figured you'd help me."

"Who was it turned you out?" North demanded.

"There was near a dozen busted in on me. Men from Texas. I didn't know them."

"But you took their money to sell out, knowing we'd starve to pay for your treachery," North snarled. He thrust his hand into the pocket of the heavy coat which he had stripped off McQueen, pulled it out with a thick wad of bills clutched tight, and riffled through them.

"Here's what they paid you—blood money. And now you were figurin' it was safe to head back and have a look. *Where's that grub cached?*"

McQueen shrank back, attempting no denial.

"I—I don't know," he gurgled. "They just took it—"

North hit him across the mouth, a blow which brought blood to smashed lips.

"It won't be far off," he said shrewdly. "Lead us to it!"

"I tell you I can't—I don't know—"

"Doll," North instructed, "find a couple of stones. We'll strip him and tie him fast, head and feet. And leave him there."

McQueen's eyes dilated.

"I—I'll show you," he shrieked. "They'll kill me—but I'll show you."

"Make sure you do," North warned grimly. "For we'll sure kill you if you don't."

They found the cache, as North had suspected, less than an hour away. Here was an old cabin in the brakes, well hidden; stocked now with the food and supplies which had been at the post, with several wagons which had been used for transport concealed not far away. A quick survey showed that the store had been well stocked.

There were four other men inside the cabin, crouching about a big stove, fuzzed with liquor and inertia. One of them was Karth.

The surprise was complete. So much so that there was no resistance. North looked at them and shrugged.

"Let them go," he instructed. "They can even have a gun between them if they want—but no horses. And no food. They didn't aim for us to have any. But if you should live, Karth, keep out of my way. Next time, I'll finish what I started back in Texas."

Food. Here was an ample supply now to last them through the rest of the drive, extra wagons, blankets in plenty, warm clothing for men shivering and threadbare. North was silent a long while, looking back, before he gave the order to move ahead again, the next morning. Doll could guess what he was thinking. Pleasant was back there. If they had found this cache a little sooner—

But they were going on, as North had promised. And now, as if relenting, the wind shifted to a new quarter. It was raw, but it held warmth cradled in its chill. By mid-forenoon it was definite. Chinook!

The snow was graying, sinking, beginning to form puddles. Grass began to emerge. The sun shone fitfully, water was running. New life crept back into the cattle. It infected the men like a potent virus.

"We'll reach Kansas," North repeated. "When the grass grows green, we'll be there with it!"

108

- 22 -

THE PAUNCHY marshal checked in his stride, and his pock-marked face grew dour. A certain habitual jauntiness seemed gone from the walk of the man approaching along the street, but there was no mistaking the man himself. Wherever he might be, he stood out like a roan steer among a herd of red ones. The marshal lifted a hand.

"You back in town!" he growled.

Tripp Devero stopped. He looked at the marshal without really seeing him, his mind elsewhere.

"Yeah, I'm back," he agreed. "A bad egg can take a lot of settin' on without hatchin'."

"We've had too many bad eggs in St. Louis," the marshal said bluntly. "I was hopin' I'd seen the last of you, last fall."

Devero's face showed a momentary gleam of the old devil-may-care impulse.

"Now ain't that a coincidence!" he drawled. "I was hopin' just exactly the same thing—about you!"

"We been tightenin' up here," the minion of the law added, choking down his wrath. "No packin' of guns allowed in town any more. Hand over that hogleg you're wearin'. When you get ready to pull your freight, you can tell around and pick it up."

Devero hesitated, then shrugged. He had other and bigger things on his mind, and what difference did it make? There was no point in quarreling with this pompous man who strutted behind a tin shield.

"Suit yourself," he agreed, and handed it over. "But take good care of it. I'll be wantin' it one of these days."

"The sooner the better," the marshal nodded. He started to turn away, swung back on an afterthought.

"You'll be safer, this way," he added. "Not gettin' yourself into trouble. After what you did, last time you was here, I'd sure have to run you in, you comin' back. Only you had better luck 'n what you deserved."

"Luck? I could stand to hear about some of that," Devero said idly.

"You ain't got Pete Hartse's blood on yore hands, like we

109

figgered," the marshal explained. "Sure thought he was dead. . . . But he s'prised folks and got well."

That was news, and. considering it, Devero hesitated, half minded to request his gun back again. Then he shrugged. The only way to get it, of course, would be to take it away from the marshal, and that would unjug trouble. And at the moment he had no desire for more of that. He turned and went on, climbing the stairs presently to the second floor of a hotel, pausing before the door of a room with southern exposure. Judy opened to his knock, then discreetly withdrew.

Marian was seated in a chair by the window, and she turned with a smile at his entrance—a wan ghost of the look which had once brightened her face. Devero's grin was wide, but it too seemed to lack something of its old-time quality.

"That streak of sunshine sure makes you look prettier'n a crocus just poppin' its head above the snow," he said approvingly. "You feelin' better today, eh?"

"Hello, Tripp," she said, and listlessness dragged in the words. "You always say such nice things."

"That's because I have such a nice gal to say them to." He tossed his hat toward a corner, drew up another chair, and his eyes were anxious. "Maybe you ought to get outside, in the real sun. Might do you good."

"I'd like to," Marian agreed. "Only I just don't feel up to it. You've been awfully good to me, Tripp. A lot better than I deserve. I don't know what's the matter with me. But I just can't seem to take any interest in—in anything."

"It's not your fault," he said. "You've been pretty sick. One of these days we'll have you singin' like the old-time Thrush again."

She smiled but made no answer, her hands white and slender in her lap. Devero looked out the window to conceal his own anxiety. She had recovered, so far as a medico could do anything for her. But not even the return to St. Louis had had any appreciable effect. Only that morning the doctor had confessed his helplessness.

"It's a queer case," he had admitted. "A strange fever to begin with, which dragged her down physically. But there's more than that to it. I suppose you could call it an illness of the mind. Some of my colleagues would say I'm crazy, that there is no such thing. But that's the way it seems to me.

110

And I don't know what to do for it. She needs something to rouse her—to get her to take an interest in living again. She *could* do things if she wanted to—" He lifted his hands in resignation.

Devero blamed himself. She had been the old, flaming Marian when he had entered that cook house on the scarred bank of the Arkansas. All that he had wanted was a kiss, and it had never occurred to him that she could care about Rawe North or anything that he had save his possessions. It looked as if he had been wrong all the way.

The illness which had been descending upon her then had of course been partially responsible for her fainting in his arms and the long unconsciousness which had followed. But what he had done must have made it worse. She had been so excited, had reacted so violently, that the effects still persisted. And now—

He looked out the window. Dirty snow was melting, forming little puddles in the street. The winter was well advanced, and it was a warm day here in town. But St. Louis had had no effect upon her. Nothing seemed to help.

"I heard a piece of news that might interest you," he volunteered. "Seems I didn't shoot as straight as I figured, last time I was in town. Anyway, Pete Hartse fooled everybody by getting well."

She looked up quickly, really interested this time.

"He—he recovered?" she whispered. "Everybody thought he was dead, that night."

"Yeah. He looked it, all right. The marshal was just tellin' me about him, though, so I guess it's straight."

"I'm—glad," Marian said softly. "Glad that you didn't kill him, I mean, Tripp."

Devero rubbed at his chin.

"Things sure get mixed up, don't they?" he commented. "If I hadn't drilled him, he'd have finished North about half a second later. And then you wouldn't have traveled the way you did, and maybe you wouldn't have got sick at all. And the way it is—"

He shook his head, allowing the words to trail off to silence. Marian had already lapsed into her usual apathy, her brief flash of interest gone. That was what worried him, as it did the doctor. She'd ought to be able to get up and do

111

things, go out in the sunshine on a day like this. But she was almost as helpless as a baby. She had walked from her bed in the next room to this chair, but leaning heavily on the arm of Judy. It was beyond him.

Reports coming in from the west were disturbing. It was a hard winter, out on the Kansas prairies, one of the worst in many years. One storm after another, bitter cold. Big Ben was a good man, of course, and he'd do all that was humanly possible to look after the ranch and the herds. But Devero knew that he ought to be there himself. He'd been away, most of the time now, for going on half a year.

Yet how could he go away and leave Marian here, in such shape? He felt responsible for her, and he had to look after her. At least, he was doing all that he could, the best he knew. If only it would do some good!

She had said that she liked to have him sit with her. But beyond that she seemed to take little interest. He had tried to talk to her about a variety of subjects, hoping to find something which would rouse her to interest. But beyond an occasional brief flash, nothing seemed able to penetrate the lethargy that had taken possession of her. Even that news about Pete Hartse—

Speak of the devil! The door was opening behind them, with a sort of stealthy lack of sound, and he turned to see Hartse bulking huge in the doorway.

Sickness had had little effect upon the saloon keeper. While it had played havoc with his possessions, causing the closing of the Paddle Wheel, the scattering abroad of those who had contributed to his wealth, it had not made much difference physically. Once he had started to recover, his tremendous vitality had put him back on his feet as it would have with the grizzly bear he so much resembled. If he had lost any weight, he had regained it in the interval.

His eyes, small and reddish again like those of the bear, roved from one to the other as he stepped inside and closed the door. Devero came to his feet, watchful, but with sudden hope growing in him. Maybe this would rouse Marian!

Marian was looking at Hartse, quick-breathing, her eyes widening. But after a darting look at her, Hartse centered his attention on Devero.

"So you're back in town!" he growled. "The marshal was just tellin' me he'd seen you!"

And that's why you've got nerve enough to come here! Devero thought. *That shadow of the law barks at your signal—and he's told you he took my gun!*

Aloud he said, his voice indifferent:

"Old home week, ain't it? Did you want somethin', Hartse?"

"There's two things I come for." Having satisfied himself that the marshal had informed him correctly, Hartse allowed his gaze to shift to Marian, his eyes boldly appraising. "One thing, now that you're back in town, girl, you can come back to your old job. I'm openin' up again."

A faint pulse of color flowed in Marian's pale cheeks. A hand fluttered toward her throat.

"That's nice of you, Pete. Only I—I couldn't. I've been sick. I—I couldn't sing—"

"You need me to look after you—which I'm aimin' to do," Hartse growled. "I'll soon have you perky as ever." He swung his regard back to Devero.

"That's one thing I come here for. The other's to settle with you—you damned interferin' cow nurse!"

Belatedly Devero understood what he had in mind, the cold ruthlessness of the man which had made him a power along the riverfront—a power successfully challenged only the one time, and then by him. Hartse was neither the man to forget nor forgive.

It might be the new rule in this town that men were not to pack guns. A good rule to enforce against outlanders. From the moment that Hartse had entered the room Devero had observed, without surprise, that it did not apply to him. He bossed the man who pretended to administer the law, and a forty-five swung openly in his holster. And now, with the cold deliberateness of a crouching puma preparing to pounce, Hartse was dragging at his iron.

A scream tore in Marian's throat, but she was too far away, even had she been able to do anything. Hartse had come here to kill a man, and he was going about it as he had always done with such chores, without hesitation or squeamishness. It could be that his sickness had slowed his speed a little, but not much. And in this case he had no great need for haste.

Or so he figured it. Therein lay Devero's only chance. He had given up his holstered gun at the marshal's demand, but he was too old a hand to go around gun-naked. He carried a hide-out weapon, and now, late though it was, he tried to get it out. Knowing even as he did so that he would be too slow, against the cold treachery aimed against him.

Marian was screaming, or it might have been the echo of her first wild cry. Devero was not sure. For gun-blasting was loud above it, and he staggered to the shock of a heavy bullet, poised a desperate moment and was twisted down as by a giant hand. Even then, the smoking muzzle of Hartse's gun was turning to center on him again, the face behind it as coldly malignant as that of a rattlesnake.

With a supreme effort of faltering muscles, Devero had his own gun clear. He did not bother to raise it, merely tipped the muzzle up and squeezed the trigger. He saw the sudden splinter in the floor where Hartse's second bullet struck, just in front of his face, and then, as his own gun grew too heavy to hold, he noticed that Hartse, wobbling upon his feet, was going down with a crash to shake the floor. Always he seemed to fall that way, fighting back even in death.

Shrieks were still tearing in her throat—gasping cries which almost choked her. But now Marian was upon her feet and running across the room, then to drop down and pillow the head of Tripp Devero in her lap, while his blood stained her dress.

- 23 -

THE CIMARRON had been in flood. Melting snows, hurried on by another chinook wind which blew across the plains and wiped the land clean again. A thousand tributaries poured their offering to the river, and the flood ran strong. Two men died and two hundred head of cattle were swept away in the crossing, but what was either one or the other? Nothing of consequence, so far as North was concerned, once they were on the far shore.

For now the snow was gone, and there was no other stream of consequence lying between them and their destination. It had been an epic fray, this of men and cattle against the winter. No man of them all but had suffered, with pinched cheeks and frost-bitten ears and nose, frozen fingers and toes. North's own ears had swollen as though like a moose he was sprouting antlers out from his head, and they had been tender to the touch for weeks, peeling away in chunks.

But his indomitable will had driven them on—men and cattle alike. Of the seven thousand head with which he had left Texas, sixty-six hundred were coming to the grass along the Arkansas, and their increase would far more than make up the loss. A handful of men had died, or disappeared—no one had ever seen anything of the trio whom he had dispatched after Karth, with orders to bring him back or not return themselves. They had not returned.

Now at last spring was greening the land again, a faint flush of color which ran up the slopes and dipped in darker color in the draws. Sprinkled with the advance host of flowers which lifted prodigal heads to the warming sun. Grass to set the gaunted herd half mad with its taste, but interspersed with plenty of old grass from the year before to put meat back on their ribs.

Plenty of men had said it couldn't be done. That every one of them, on four feet or two, would die before the winter gave way reluctantly to spring. Plenty among his own crew. Well, he'd shown them! He was Rawe North, and this herd, this drive back to the Rail Road Track, was only a small part of his plan. The biggest part still lay ahead, and because of that nothing had stopped him, or was going to.

There was a settlement to be made—here on the banks of the flood-fed Arkansas! A settlement, and the winter had hardened his mood for the making of it.

Here was deeper green—rich and succulent now, where the fire had swept. A fair land in the warming sun, for as far as the eye could reach, and his—all his! And what was not his already he would take!

"Let the herd go," North instructed. "They can drift as they please for a while—it won't be far, on clear grass such as this."

That was true enough. Here, where the fire had cleaned

115

out the old, was all Rail Road range. They would stay on its unmixed freshness of their own accord.

"We've got other work to do," North added. "A few things to settle. After that we'll round them up and put my brand on them. But that can wait."

The other could have waited, but there was a thirst in North. It had been building in him since the day he had paused to survey the black desolation which marked where his empire had run. It was that anticipation of vengeance which had kept him going when everything seemed hopeless. Now the time was at hand.

"Those of you who want to be paid off can go," North told his crew. "But I told you when I hired you that there'd be a job here, at double pay. It's up to you."

Almost without exception they hated him. That hate had been born of cold and hardship along the trail, nourished when there was nothing else to cling to. But along with the hate was a grudging admiration. He was a hard man, Rawe North, but only a hard man could have brought them through. Likewise, their destiny was bound up with his now. They knew it without needing to be reminded of it. None of them could go back to Texas. Here it was better to work for him at double pay than to go off alone. There might be others that they would run into, men who would remember.

North deigned to explain.

"Some of you thought I was high-handed, down in Texas," he said. "But what I'm going to do here is only taking back my own. Last fall this land was black, where it's pure green now—because I'd been burned out. My herds had been stolen, my men killed or chased off or bought. So what I'm going to do now is settle for that. Pay them back in a way they'll understand. When I get through I'll be boss of about half of Kansas. Those who ride with me won't need to worry about what's behind them."

That was big talk. But it appealed to them. Far better to work for a man who could back what he said, back them when it might be necessary. North had been given some unpleasant lessons, but he had profited by them.

"We'll start riding in the morning," he added. "That's all."

For the first time since he had set out for St. Louis with

116

the summer sun hot overhead, he rode back to his old head-
quarters. The land was green now, warm with the unfolding
promise of the spring. For all that, it was still a melancholy
prospect. The cook house stood as it had been left, but no
man had been near the place for a long while. Weeds had
sprung up to hide the scars where the big new house and
the other buildings had gone down in ruin, but lack of them
was like a blot against the landscape.

He splashed his horse across and up to the door, then dismounted and entered. There was the shattered chair on the
floor, a sense of confusion in the room. He looked about for
a moment, puzzled, then with growing incredulity. Here was
a glove, lying on the edge of a bunk, a glove which he had
seen times enough. He picked it up, ran it through his fingers uncertainly, and seemed to thrill to a touch of old fire.
Marian Breen's!

There was no doubt of it. A faint intangible perfume still
lingered on the glove, as though she had been in this room.
Here were other small evidences that she had lived in this
house. Long ago, somehow, which meant that she had come
on here, despite the burned-over ground. Seeing it, knowing
what it meant, she had not turned back. She had come here,
had waited for him—

Then what had happened? There was the broken chair,
the evidences of struggle, of hasty departure. Nothing more.
None of his crew, nor any others, had been here during the
winter. But she had come on, and had waited for him! And
he had not returned.

It was in a grimmer, more savage mood that North rode
back to join the crew. He'd looked forward to what had to
be done with anticipation. Now there was something in his
air which caused the others to look and draw away. But no
man questioned him.

He had sent Doll on ahead, days before. Doll was a
changed man from the hot-head who had ridden south with
winter at his back. A man grown dour and taciturn as North
himself, but, as always, dependable. He had not said whether
or not he liked the job given him, but he had gone without
comment. Now he returned.

"There's five of the old crew workin' for Devero now,"

he reported. "Tate, Van Gordy, Squint, Larrigan and Sneezy. That's all I could find."

"Five?" North frowned in surprise. "But that's only a handful. There ought to be a score, at least."

Doll shrugged.

"Five is all," he repeated.

"We'll find the rest of them—somewhere, sooner or later," North promised. "Else they'll travel far from Kansas. What else?"

"I've ridden across a good bit of Devero's range. And talked to several men. He's got a good calf crop. And his herd wintered through. But he only has seven thousand head of stock, otherwise."

"Seven thousand? But he stole my herd—besides his own. Where are they? And where the blazes is he? What's he been up to?"

"I wouldn't know," Doll said woodenly. "He hasn't been around all winter. Report has it he went back to St. Louis."

North swore.

"He would, damn him!" he gritted. "Well, once this job's done, I'll hunt him down, if it's the last thing I do!"

Doll asked no questions. North fired another at him.

"You didn't find out anything else?"

"That's about all. You said not to talk to anybody that would know me. But there's something funny here."

North disregarded that.

"Tell the men to saddle," he instructed. "I'm not waitin' for morning. They struck in the dark—and it's a good idea."

Midnight, and a half-moon hovering hawk-like. There was just enough light to see the bedded herds of Tripp Devero, where they spread wide in full-fed content. Only the moon and a ranging coyote was about to see them stirred to startled action, a vast herd gradually rounded up and set in motion, across toward the land which North claimed for his own. The smell of dawn was in the air, a moist dawn pregnant with bursting buds and etched with bird-song, when the whole bunch was well under way.

"Keep them going," North instructed, and swung the bulk of his crew back. "Now we'll really get at work."

A startled meadow lark soared to flight, away from the pounding hoofs of half a hundred horses as they thundered

118

past. One light had appeared in the window of the cook shack, a tremulous streamer of smoke was lifting against the lingering dark. Otherwise the place drowsed as the avengers swept down. This, North reflected grimly, would be an eye for an eye.

Everything was coming his way at last. It had been a long grind and a hard one, but his parents had named him well. He was Rawe North, and no one could stand in his way. This was the beginning of settlement. He savored it as he rode.

The surprised crew put up a fight, but from the outset they had no chance. That was the way he'd planned it. Guns sharp in the shattered dawn, overwhelming force. Some of Devero's men escaped, and he let them go, merely making sure that they were chased so that they would not stop. Of those who remained to fight, the five who had once taken his pay were among them. North was watchful for that.

Two of them, along with others of their comrades, died with their boots on. It was unseasonably early for hail, but there was a leaden rain of it this morning. The other three, along with the remaining part of the crew, sullenly surrendered.

North gestured.

"You can have two choices," he said. "Work for me—or get out of the country. Except for these three!" He gestured again, to where cottonwoods grew tall. "Hang them!"

He turned his back to their pleas and protests, then paused for one afterthought. The new house had been rising, was nearing completion. A structure of graceful sweep such as his own had been, the fall before.

"Burn it," North ordered. And the drifting smoke of it was in his nostrils as he turned away. So that he knew he should have been content. But, strangely enough, his mood was more savage than ever, so that his cayuse leaped to the goad of the spurs.

For a couple of days he threw himself into the work to be done—the branding of these vast herds which now ranged on his acres, corraled under his Rail Road iron. The order was the same in every case. Never mind what brand they wore to begin with. Put his on them, slit their ears in the lop of the Jingle Bob.

119

Sound arose endlessly from thousands of throats as the disturbed herd was handled. Bawling which grew hoarse and strained, ebbing after midnight, only to begin with full vigor as the new day came with the riders about their task. Music to the ears of any cattleman.

But in the ears of Rawe North it was only a din. He gestured impatiently, swung to Doll.

"There's nothing to do here," he said. "The boys can do this as well as we can. Pack your duffle. We're startin' for the railroad in the morning. It's quicker."

Doll, obeying in silence, had no need to ask what their destination would be. He knew. St. Louis.

- 24 -

FATE, Devero was discovering, had a way of playing pranks. Or maybe, as some others did, he should call it luck. In any event, it was putting on the same sort of scene which had been played in this room some weeks before, but in reverse.

Now it was he who sat in the chair in the sunlight, still pale and thin, while Marian hovered anxiously about him and worried because his recovery was so slow. Though the doctor insisted that he was lucky to be alive at all.

"A forty-five bullet, my dear, is nothing to toy with," the man of medicine had declaimed. "The knock-down power of it is simply terrific, the killing power little less. And he took a bad wound. Only a strong man would recover from that at all."

Well, he was recovering, though his legs were still as uncertain as those of a new-born calf. And there had, perhaps, been some good out of that murderous shot of Hartse's. The bullet which had struck Devero down had had the effect upon the Golden-Throated Thrush which both he and the medico had hoped something might accomplish.

His sickness had roused her out of that deadly lethargy, and since then she had nursed him back toward health, taking no thought for herself. There had been long vigils when he hovered close between life and death. Only her presence, the touch of her cool hand on his fevered head, had been

120

able to draw him back from the brink. But in the process she seemed to have recovered her own old vitality and interest in life, and so, he figured, it was cheap at the price.

Feet were upon the stairs outside, a knock sounded on the door. Marian opened it, and gave a little cry of surprise and welcome at sight of the man who stood there. Bud Farris. But a changed Bud. Tanned and husky again, fiddling his hat in his hands. If one eye looked out at the world more blankly than the other, there was nothing outwardly to indicate it.

"I—uh—yore foreman, Big Ben, he asked me to come an' see how you was gettin' along—an' bring you a message," Farris explained. "Last fall, Tripp, you told him to try and find out what had happened to North's big herd. So he—"

Devero glanced warningly at Marian.

"Not now—" he began, but Marian interposed quickly.

"Right now, Bud. I want to hear this. What *did* happen to Mr. North's herd?"

"Well—it took Ben quite a while to find out, for sure," Farris explained. "Course, it was plain enough that whoever had rustled them and burned the range had worked to lay the blame on you, Tripp. I—uh—I figured that about you myse'f, from what I'd overheard some of 'em say when they struck. That is, till I got to know you better."

"Go on," Marian urged.

"Well, it turns out it was just a case of a man who hated North and aimed to get even with him and have his herd," Farris explained. "And he was clever enough to work it to lay the blame on somebody else—you, as it happened. Big Ben found that out. Learned who it was. A man named Zip— he and a twin brother of his hated North for somethin' from long back."

"And he hated me," Devero said quietly. "I helped bust up a ring of rustlers that they headed, once. Another brother of theirs got strung up in the process. They were too speedy."

"That it, eh? Well, Big Ben found who it'd been. And he followed a cold trail of that rustled herd for two-three hundred miles, over into the Colorado country. He was just about losin' all trace and ready to give it up as a bad job when he met up with a Mexican named Pedro Gonzales. And this Pedro, he knew about that herd. Fact is, he told

121

Ben of a place not too far off that everybody in that part of the country had taken to callin' the Valley of Death."

"How come?"

"Pedro said he'd show Ben. So he took him there. Ben says it was easy to see why—though the sight near turned his stomach. There were black specks in the sky, same as there'd been above that place for weeks. Vultures. And more of 'em on the ground, so gorged they could hardly fly. And bones—bones and horns. Accordin' to Ben, it wasn't a pretty place, with whitenin' skeletons of that herd as far as the eye could reach. That was where a lot of North's bunch ended up—there in that valley."

"But what on earth happened to them?" Marian gasped. "Why should such a herd die? Did they starve?"

Farris shook his head.

"Nope. That was what Ben asked Pedro. But there was plenty grass—and water enough. And they died before winter hit. Pedro said it was the hand of God, a judgment upon the evil men who would do this thing. But Ben, bein' a cattleman, and practical, he figured out what had hit them. Blackleg."

"Blackleg?" Devero half rose up from his chair, then sank back again.

"Yeah. Pedro said that when they first died, you could run yore hand down the leg of one, and it'd crackle like paper. And they died by the thousands. Ben said it was better luck than Rawe North deserved, whether he knew it or not."

"Luck? For North? I don't see how he figured that out," Marian protested. "After all, it was his herd—and he lost them."

"Sure he did," Farris conceded. "But like Big Ben says, the bunch must have had the germs of that blackleg in them before ever they left the Arkansas. Workin' in their blood, gettin' ready to bust out. Funny how things like that'll work, sometimes. Keepin' them on the move after they was stolen spread it through the whole herd, of course, and made it twice as bad a killer, likely." He shook his head.

"But the point is this. Even if they'd been left alone, it would still have broken out, of course. And then it'd not only have wiped out North's bunch, but would have spread

122

across to yore herd as well, Tripp. But the bad thing then is that it'd have been in the earth, so that cattle couldn't be grazed safe on that range for a dozen years. This way, since nothin's happened to your stock this winter, Tripp—least, nothin' had when I left there—why, it looks like the plague missed them. So, if North only knew it, havin' his sick bunch drove off his range that way was a lucky break for him in the long run."

Marian was looking, not at Farris, but at Devero. He reddened uncomfortably under her gaze.

"The big thing," she said, "is that you had nothing to do with it, Tripp. You wouldn't bother to deny it, would you—not even to me. You were too proud for that. But somehow I knew all along that you'd never stoop to fight that way."

"Well, I brought word, like Ben asked me to," Farris added. "I got to be going now. Got some other business to tend to."

He went out, and they heard his boots going down the stairs. Then coming back up again, as though he had forgotten something. This time he didn't bother to knock. For a moment, neither looked. Then Marian spun about suddenly, and her hand went to her throat. It was not Bud Farris who stood there now, but Rawe North.

- 25 -

NORTH's gaze went from one of them to the other, to the gaunted face of Devero, the flush on Marian's, and his look grew more dour. Carefully he closed the door behind him.

"Heard I'd find you here, Devero," he said, "and figured you'd be around, Marian. It's been a long trail—since last fall. But I'd have followed it if it'd led me straight to hell itself."

Some of the old mocking note crept back into Devero's voice.

"From your looks, North, you might have come from there."

"I have," North agreed grimly. "After last fall, I traveled to Texas, and then back to the Arkansas with seven thousand head of beef. Drivin' through the worst winter that country's seen in half a century. But I brought them back, Marian. I didn't lose any time—not a day. I promised you an empire, that you'd be the wife of a rich man. I keep my promises. Maybe I made a mistake, leavin' you to look after yourself. I figured you'd turn right back when you found I'd been wiped out. But I did it all for you. And now I'm back again, bigger than ever."

The old arrogance was in his voice, the cold challenge in his eyes. He had been well named. North. There was only coldness in him, nothing of warmth. If ever there had been, that had been squeezed out somewhere along those winter trails. Looking at him, half understanding, Marian felt a sudden rush of pity.

"I did stay, Rawe," she said gently. "I waited for you— on what was your land. I would have married you if you had come."

North swallowed. Here was confirmation of what he had guessed, but he could no more understand it than when he had discovered that glove which whispered of her presence, there in that shattered room. And what he could not understand served always to make him uncomfortable.

"I—I found your glove—where you'd been there," he blurted. "Just the other day."

Marian nodded, her eyes seeming to see beyond him, back to that barren country.

"I waited," she repeated. "But you didn't come, Rawe. I would have married you, then. But not now. Now I'm going to marry Tripp."

Devero looked up, startled. She had been very good to him, in these weeks of illness. But for her care, the long hours of patient nursing, he guessed that he wouldn't be here now. But he had kept a tight rein on himself, saying nothing. She was paying back a debt, as she viewed it. That, and pity, would account for all this. And he was no man to trespass on the pity of anyone.

North's face had been puzzled. Now it seemed sardonic.

"So you've changed your mind, eh?" he mocked. "You figure now that it's Devero who's the big man on the Arkansas?"

Marian recoiled as if he had struck her, her face whitening, then it flamed with color.

124

"You fool!" she cried, and then her mood changed again, with something like compassion in her eyes. "I'm sorry, Rawe," she added, more quietly. "But I can see now that you'll never understand."

"Won't I, ma'am?" Angry color was in North's face to match her own. "Don't delude yourself. I understand only too well. You made it plain from the day I first knew you that you were out to get the best bargain you could—and I've lived up to my part of our compact! But don't make a mistake. Maybe Devero was the big man for a while last fall. You should have married him then. He isn't any longer. What he had is gone, as completely as what I had was destroyed half a year ago. I settle accounts—and I've settled this one—all but the final payment. I'm a bigger man on the Arkansas than I was last fall. Everything that you've wanted I can give you. He can't give you anything."

He stopped, breathless, baffled by the look in Marian's eyes. Such a look as he had never seen there before. A glance, once more, of pity or compassion.

"I suppose I shouldn't blame you for taking me at my word, Rawe," she said. "For not understanding. You're what you are, and nothing can ever change that. And I did tell you that I would marry the man who could give me the most, didn't I?"

"Yes," he agreed hoarsely. "You made that plain."

"That was my fault," Marian sighed. "You see—well, I'll try and be honest with you—both of you. I liked you both. In fact, each of you attracted me—just as I seemed to appeal to you. You were the only two men who ever did mean anything to me. Both of you were strong, ruthless, and the kind who did things. You were cattle kings on the Arkansas.

"Maybe you can't understand what that meant to me. I—I'd had a hard life. A rigorous upbringing. I was one of a big family. All that we ever had at home was poverty. Never quite enough to eat—never enough of anything. I made up my mind that I was going to get what I wanted out of life, without making a fool of myself. My mother had married for love—I guess. Certainly not for money. But I didn't believe in love. I wasn't going to be fooled by any of the usual traps. The only rule that counted was to get what you could, to do the best you could for yourself."

She paused for a moment. North's face had not changed.

"It's a good rule," he said. "That's what I liked about you."

"I suppose so," she agreed. "But there's something else, curious as it may seem, that I still believed in. Loyalty. I went out to Kansas with you to marry you, Rawe. That was why I waited. I intended to keep my promise."

He stared at her, uncertain now.

"When you knew I didn't have anything—" He stopped, remembering the glove. Stubborn anger grew in him again.

"What does it matter?" he asked. "I'm here now. And with something to offer you again."

Marian shook her head.

"No," she denied. "Not with anything to offer me, Rawe. Not any more. All that you have is in your corral—the bigger the better. But it isn't in you."

"Words," he flung at her, bitterly. "I didn't think you were the kind to smother a man with words. I don't understand you."

"No, I don't suppose you do," she agreed. "And I'm sorry, Rawe. I truly am. What I'm trying to tell you is—that I'm only a woman, after all. And I've found out that there is such a thing as love. And that it counts for more, is bigger than all the rest."

North was like a grizzly, hemmed in by yapping dogs which snarled and bit from half a dozen directions. Angry, baffled, growing more furious as he began to comprehend.

"You sound like a fool," he said roughly. "But you're the only woman for me. And don't you understand? Devero's wiped out. I've treated him as he treated me. He hasn't a thing left—not a building standing, no cattle on his grass. I'm even takin' over that range. I'm not one of the two big men on the Arkansas any longer. I've played your own game, Devero, and beat you at it. I'm the only man on the Arkansas now!"

For answer, Marian turned, crossed the room to Devero again, and rested her hand lightly on his shoulder. There was still pity in her eyes and the tones of her voice.

"I feel sorry for you, Rawe," she said. "Really I do. That a man so big in some ways should be so blind."

126

Fury burst out of him at last, but it was a controlled rage, cold and calculating.

"So that's the way it is?" he gibed. "He's been here with you till he's hoodwinked you completely! Well, no man can say that I was ever a piker. I'll gamble with you, Devero—all or nothing! A roll of the dice, a game of cards. You name it. If I win, she marries me, goes back. If you win—you can go back with her, and everything on the western river is yours!"

Devero had listened, mostly silent, almost a spectator to this which had enmeshed the three of them from the beginning. His blood stirred again in the old wild way to North's challenge, but he shook his head.

"No," he said. "For a ranch, yes, I'd gamble you, North. For anything else on earth, I'd take you on. But for her—no."

"Then you're a bigger fool than I thought you were." The rage blared like an off-key trumpet in North's voice now, so much so that he failed to hear the door open again behind him.

"Why do you think I made such an offer, Devero?" North raged on. "Only because I aimed to beat you. I promised myself long ago to settle with you—and most of it's been done. Now I'm finishin' the job. Looks like you've no gun. But I pack two. Take one. And the winner takes all!"

Tripp Devero was still a sick man, slow and unready of movement. That was plain to see. But North was past all caring. He tossed a gun across the room, to fall at Devero's feet. And in almost a continuing part of the same motion his hand chopped down toward his holster, his other weapon was a flash in the afternoon sunlight slanting across the floor.

Marian screamed, the sound swallowed in gun-thunder. Then she stared with dilating eyes from Doll, who lounged in the doorway, smoking revolver in hand, to North, sinking down almost as Pete Hartse had done upon another occasion, his unfired gun still clutched in stiffening fingers. Devero, though trying hard, had not been able to reach the gun on the floor. He had all but fallen from his chair in the effort.

127

Regret was in the face of Noland Doll as he returned his own weapon to holster.

"I'm right sorry it had to be that way, ma'am," he apologized. "And he was my friend. . . . But you see, Miss Breen, I met another lady, down in Texas, last fall. She said you were the only friend she ever had. Altie, her name was." He pronounced it softly, like a benediction.

"Altie died—takin' a bullet that would have killed him." He nodded toward North. "And the last thing she ever said, just about, was to ask him to be good to you, ma'am—to make you happy. Seemed like he was forgettin' that—and so—on her account—I had to do it."

He hesitated, added a last word.

"I reckon you will be, ma'am—and that'd sure please her. She thought a lot of you."

Nodding, he turned and went out and down the stairs, a man walking with eyes that looked on empty places. For a moment, then, it seemed to Tripp Devero that Marian was going to faint again, so he got quickly to his feet and gathered her into his arms.

THE END

www.ingramcontent.com/pod-product-compliance
Lightning Source LLC
Chambersburg PA
CBHW022033170626
46808CB00003B/1174